The Return of Skeleton Man

Also by Joseph Bruchac

SKELETON MAN

THE DARK POND

WHISPER IN THE DARK

The Return of Skeleton Man

JOSEPH BRUCHAC

Illustrations by Sally Wern Comport

HARPERCOLLINS*PUBLISHERS*

The Return of Skeleton Man

 For information address HarperCollins Children's Books, a division of HarperCollins Publishers, 1350 Avenue of the Americas, New York, NY 10019.
www.harperchildrens.com

Library of Congress-in-Publication Data

Bruchac, Joseph, date

The return of Skeleton Man / Joseph Bruchac ; illustrations by Sally Wern Comport.— 1st ed.

p. cm.

Sequel to: Skeleton Man.

Summary: When Molly and her parents attend a conference at Mohonk Mountain House, Molly begins to fear that she is being watched by the very man who kidnapped and tried to kill them all the previous year.

ISBN-10: 0-06-058090-9 (trade bdg.)

ISBN-13: 978-0-06-058090-2 (trade bdg.)

ISBN-10: 0-06-058091-7 (lib. bdg.) — ISBN-13: 978-0-06-058091-9 (lib. bdg.)

[1. Psychopaths—Fiction. 2. Mohawk Indians—Fiction. 3. Indians of North America—New York (State)—Fiction. 4. Mohonk Mountain House—Fiction.] I. Comport, Sally Wern, ill. II. Title.

PZ7.B82816Ret 2006 2005022891
[Fic]—dc22 CIP
AC

---

3 4 5 6 7 8 9 10

❖

First Edition

Contents

Contents

Prologue

I hate sequels. I know that some kids love them, but not me. Once a story is over I'd just like it to be done with. Finis, as my teacher, Ms. Shabbas, puts it. But every time you go to a movie these days it seems like half the stuff showing is either sequels or sequels of sequels or even, like in those newer Star Wars films, prequels. All that ever gets better are the special effects. I ask you, though: After you've seen one planet blown up, what can you do to top that? I want to say "Give me a break!" to those producers and directors. "Do something new."

The horror movies, of course, are the worst. *Halloween Part 2006. Friday the 13th Times Infinity.* It seems as if no matter what those sappy kids do to get rid of one of those mad-dog monsters like Freddy or Jason, he just comes back. You can shoot him, stab him, cut his head off, bury him, burn him, run him through a blender, make him into muffins, and nuke him in your microwave. It doesn't matter. There he is again, all knifey and bloodthirsty and ready to throw more buckets of gore in the petrified protagonist's face. You can even send Jason off to Hades and he'll still reappear—to fight Freddy in outer space or something equally weird. Once again, give me a break.

You might think I'm saying that sequels are boring and unrealistic. Well, they are. That was pretty much the way I used to think about them. But I have to confess it is more than that for me now. What bothers me most about sequels now is not the thought that they're unrealistic. It's the fear that maybe they're true. Maybe some monsters really are that hard to kill. Maybe, like poor old Jamie Lee Curtis, I'll be going on with my life all la-la-la-la-la, everything is fiiine. Until I turn a corner and find *him* waiting for me.

1

Arriving

"Look up there, Molly. That's Sky Top Tower."

I shift my gaze up, way up. There, far in the distance, at the top of a huge cliff, is a tall stone tower. I can hardly believe it. Here we are, on a late-autumn day, speeding along the New York State Thruway in the midst of a twenty-first-century seventy-mile-per-hour stream of traffic, dodging Winnebagos (the trucks, not the Indians) and people more interested in their cell phone conversations than in staying in their own lane, and I'm staring at something that looks like it belongs in a Dracula movie.

"Wow," I gasp. Then, just to show my parents how articulate I am, I say it again. "Wow!"

But I'm not the only one awed by the sight.

"Is that really where we're going?" my mom asks in a tone that indicates she hopes the answer is yes.

In the rearview mirror I can see the big grin that spreads over my father's face. He'd always loved to surprise us in the past, but over the last year or so, he's been avoiding springing things on Mom and me unexpectedly, which is understandable considering the recent events we barely survived. I haven't seen that wide a smile on his face for months. It makes me so happy that I wiggle in my seat like a puppy.

"Uh-huh," Dad says in that slow, confident voice of his. "That's where the conference is taking place." He carefully checks his mirrors and puts on his blinker to move into the exit lane for New Paltz. "Well, not exactly in that tower. There's a huge old Victorian hotel on that mountaintop, just below the tower, with 251 rooms."

"Cool," I say.

Dad nods. "Way cool, indeed, Molly girl. It's called the Mohonk Mountain House, and when you are up there you feel like there's no place else in the world. Totally isolated in the middle of a vast forest preserve."

"Mohonk?" my mother asks. "Isn't that where they had the Friends of the Indian conferences back in the 1880s, honey?"

I lean back to listen. It's going to be one of

those discussions between my mom and dad that's as much a seminar as a conversation. Some people might find it boring, but my dad is a natural storyteller and my mom has this way of explaining historical events that just makes them come alive for me.

I hug myself as I listen and look out the window. My dad explains that two brothers, the Smileys, started building the Mohonk Mountain House back in 1869. It began as one building, but wings got added on and it just kept getting bigger and bigger. All kinds of major events have taken place at Mohonk, starting at the end of the nineteenth century with the Friends of the Indian—who did do a lot to make things better for native people—right up to the present day. In recent years the Smiley family has added many modern facilities, from videoconferencing rooms to an Olympic-size ice-skating rink. The Mountain House restaurants are famous, and people come to the hotel from all over the world for weekend getaways. It's also a favorite place for business conferences like the seminars my father's bank is sending him to. This is his second visit but the first time we are joining him.

Their discussion pauses only when we go

through the tollbooth; then we are off the thruway. The tower is out of sight now. We're heading into the town of New Paltz, one of those places that used to be surrounded by farms but is gradually sprawling out with development. There are the usual fast-food places and chain stores, but when we drive into the town itself it gets better.

"Ambience," Mom says.

I know what she means. The buildings are old and the storefronts are all different here. They reflect the kind of stuff you see in places dominated by a big university like New Paltz—trendy little ethnic restaurants, colorful hand-painted signs, and small, unique stores.

"Walking and shopping later this weekend?" Mom says, turning back for a moment to look at me, her own smile almost as big as my dad's was.

"Def!" I say. I can already picture Mom and me strolling down the streets, the warm autumn sun shining as we window-shop or have tea at that little place there, or check out that bookstore on the corner here.

It all seems too good to be true.

We're through the town now, passing over a bridge across a little river and taking a winding road that leads up the mountain. The Smileys, whose descendants still run the place, loved nature. So they bought up thousands of acres of the Shawangunk Mountain range just to keep it wild. Then, in 1969, they turned sixty-four hundred acres of their land into the Mohonk Preserve—which surrounds the Mountain House—the biggest private nature preserve in all of New York State.

"Wow!" is going through my head again. The glaciers that sculpted the Shawangunk range made spectacular cliffs everywhere. The narrow road we're following is winding back and forth like a snake along the tops of those sheer drops. I catch a couple of glimpses of the town and the roads below, but most of the time all I can see is an endless expanse of evergreen forest. Hemlock and pine and cedar and spruce.

"Like going back into the past, isn't it?" my dad says to us. He doesn't take his eyes off the road. My dad is Mr. Safe Driver. Both hands on the wheel. "Except for this little highway, it's kind of what it was like a thousand years ago when it was just our people and the land here."

"Not our people," my mom says with a little smile. History being her thing, she can't resist the opportunity to correct him. "This area was Lenape land, not Mohawk."

"Well," Dad says, "I'll bet there were Mohawk tourists back then, too. Now, check this out. Got your passport ready, Molly?"

He nods his head toward the little building that appeared ahead of us as we rounded the turn. Of course they don't ask us for passports. That's just my dad being corny. Polite people ask where we're going and then wave us through the gate after Dad says he's going to the seminar.

"A gatehouse?" Mom says. "Where are we, Beverly Hills?"

"Better than that, small-town girl," Dad replies.

I giggle. It's fun to see Mom and Dad teasing each other like this.

"Just you wait," Dad adds. "You ain't seen nothing yet."

And, just as he promised, when we get around the next corner I see exactly what he means. Rising ahead of us are wide lawns, little open-air structures scattered all over the place, stone walls, and gardens that even now, in late autumn, look amazing. But what is really mind-boggling is the actual Mountain House. A gigantic wooden building, it seems to rise up from the cliffs themselves. It is seven stories tall and it looks like something out of a gothic story. Porches sweep along the sides as it spreads out, just going on forever. Not only that, it is right next to a beautiful lake and mirrored by sheer cliffs on the other side of it. I feel as if we have driven into a fairy tale.

Dad pulls up in front. He stops and is about to get out to give his keys to the parking attendant. But I don't give him a chance to do that. I throw my arms around his neck from the backseat and give him the biggest hug.

"This is going to be the best vacation ever," I cry.

2

The Path

I thought this path through the woods would be a shortcut. Mistake number one, because I seem to have taken a wrong turn somewhere or else the path has grown twice as long after dark as it was when I first found it before dinner. I'm not sure how much farther I have to go, and I do not have a flashlight. Mistake number two. But the moon was really bright when I left the main lodge, and I was only going to walk a little ways in the moonlight before coming back. No way did I expect that the full moon was going to go behind the big bank of clouds that came rolling up over the white stones of the Shawangunk Mountains. No way was it going to get so dark that I could barely see my hand in front of my face. No way? Way.

That was my third mistake, thinking there was no way I could get in trouble here. There's nothing threatening, nothing dangerous, nothing after me—except in my memory. It's safe here at this old, well-cared-for resort on the mountaintop. Isn't it?

I'm trying to move quietly. My steps, though, are far from quiet. Snow hasn't come yet, even though a storm that might bring a dusting of snow to the high slopes has been forecast. The dry, fallen beech leaves rustle as I walk. Thick old trees loom overhead, making this more like a tunnel than a path. Cedar twigs and cones crunch underfoot. I don't like making this much noise in the woods.

Be quiet, my father always says. *Move slow. Calm yourself down.*

So that is what I try to do. I take slower, more careful steps. I roll my feet, heel to toe, the way my father taught me. It works. I no longer sound like a three-legged moose. But now I can hear the pounding of my heart. It is so loud that it sounds like a drum. I am not calming myself down.

A song my homeroom teacher made up pops into my head:

There's nothing more fearful than fear itself,
So hang your neuroses back up on the shelf.

You'll just be more afraid the more that you
fear,
So lift up your chin and smile, my dear.

Isn't that a hideous song? But I actually find myself starting to sing it as I walk along. The moon has come out again. I can see the path ahead of me. I'm not sure how far away the big old hotel is, where my parents are waiting, but it can't be that far. I'm feeling better. I sing a little louder. It's like whistling in the dark to keep away something evil. Unless something evil likes the sound of whistling. Mistake number four.

I quickly shut my mouth. I stop walking. I've just heard the sound of something behind me. Not feet rustling through the leaves. Not the crackling of branches breaking as a heavy body thrusts its way through them. No, a far scarier sound than that. It is the dry *tschick-a-tschick* of bone against bone, accompanied by the wind-whistling sound of breath.

I turn to see a grinning skull face looming over me, its teeth dripping fresh blood. Long, bony hands reach out to grab me. I can't get away. A heart-stopping scream tears the dark fabric of the night.

3

Bad Memories

I struggle to escape from the grip of Skeleton Man's hand. But it won't let go.

"Molly," a familiar voice says. "It's all right."

That's when I realize that the hand holding my shoulder is not all cold and made of bone. Its grasp is gentle. I realize that heart-stopping scream was my own. I open my eyes and look up into my mother's concerned face.

I sit up and look around. It's not night at all. I'm not in the woods but safe inside our suite of rooms. It's only our third day here, but already it feels like home. Late-autumn sunlight is coming in through the window behind my mother's head. It shines through her hair in a way that makes it look almost like an angel's halo or the aura you see glowing around saints in old paintings. I take a deep, trembling breath and let it out. I'm remembering now. I was feeling tired after our rock climb and hike up through the Lemon Squeeze to the tower on Sky Top, so I decided to take a nap before dinner.

Mom puts her arms around me. "It was just a dream, honey," she says.

I hug her back and sit up.

"I'm okay," I say. I even manage to smile. Molly the warrior is regaining control. She's confident, pushing the other Molly, the one who is a wounded wimp, way into the background, maybe even out of the picture entirely. Or at least that is how I make it look. I know how much it hurts Mom to see me upset.

But she isn't ready to let it go yet. She studies my face. If my dad were here and not still deep in that afternoon discussion called, I kid you not, "Enron and the Perils of Accrual Accounting," he would be holding our hands in his, making our own little circle of strength. It's kind of a Mohawk Indian thing, that circle of strength idea. He learned it from his own grandparents when he was growing up on the reservation at Akwesasne, on the border between the United States and Canada.

"A circle," my father always says, "is the oldest shape and the strongest." His voice is deep and calm. "That's why we dance in a circle, just as the Rabbit People taught us to dance. When we are together in a circle, we can all see each other's faces. A real circle, a circle of love and caring and respect, can keep a family together. It can help you survive almost any threat."

My dad has always tried to pass along to me as much of our Mohawk heritage as possible, including the old stories. I've talked with my parents about those stories a lot over the past year. I'm grateful my dad told them to me because I think the lessons I learned helped me survive what I went through. There are two lessons in particular that helped me.

The first is that there really are monsters. They may have different names these days and wear different masks than in ancient times, but they can still kill you. Knowing that monsters do exist can help you recognize danger before it's too late. You'll realize you have to get out of the way and not just stand there like a fawn frozen in the middle of a four-lane highway while a semitrailer bears down on you at eighty miles an hour with its headlights blazing.

The second lesson is that even a child may be able to overcome or outwit a monster if she just keeps her wits about her and doesn't panic. Be brave and the monster may fall. That was how it was with me.

What the old stories fail to mention is the panic that comes later. When it ended, I was a mess, despite having been a heroine in the papers and featured in a spot on CNN for two days in a row: GIRL SAVES PARENTS FROM KIDNAPPER WHO POSED AS UNCLE. (Then she falls apart.)

I suppose it wasn't that bad. I am, after all, known for melodrama. It wasn't like I couldn't function on a day-to-day basis or that I got hysterical every time I heard a loud noise. It was the bad dreams. In those dreams, Skeleton Man came back to get me and there was no one there to help me, not even the rabbit.

What rabbit? I know some of you are probably asking that right now, as well as a lot of other questions. What is this crazy kid babbling about? Here I am, assuming you all know my story while I rattle on without making much sense.

That's the problem with a sequel. You need to know the backstory. I won't tell it all. But I'll hit the high points like they do on some of those TV police shows.

Previously in Molly's life I was just a normal sixth grader—if normal includes being Mohawk Indian and having a father with a Harvard MBA who works for a big bank and tells his daughter bloodcurdling old Indian tales. I have to tell you about one of those stories right now, because it is a big part of what happened to me.

That story is the one about Skeleton Man. He was a greedy, lazy uncle who sat around the fire in his longhouse all day waiting for his family to bring him food. One day, when no one was around and all the food in the pot was gone, he thought he saw something to eat that had fallen into the coals. He reached for it and burned his finger so badly that he stuck it in his mouth to cool the singed flesh. "Oooh, I have found something tasty," he said, meaning his own cooked finger.

So he ate it. Then, seeing how easy it was, he stuck his other fingers in the coals, cooked the flesh on them, and ate them one by one. But he was still hungry. So he ended up cooking his whole self until all that was left of him was a skeleton. Gross, I know, but I used to adore that story and ask my father to tell it again and again.

Then Skeleton Man, who was still hungry, lured other members of his family into the dark longhouse so he could kill them and cook them and eat them. They just went in, one by one, not realizing their relative's hunger and greed had turned him into a monster. Finally, only one little girl was left. She refused to come into the longhouse because she knew something was wrong with the one who had been her uncle. So Skeleton Man came out and began to chase her.

Tschick-a-tschick-tschick-a-tschick, that was the noise his dry bones made, rubbing together, as he pursued her. He might have caught her, but she was helped by a rabbit she had rescued from the river earlier. It led her through the darkness. It helped her keep one step ahead of the cannibal skeleton.

Finally, the rabbit showed her how to trick Skeleton Man into following her out onto a log that had fallen across the swift river like a bridge. When he was in the middle, she pushed the end of the log into the water. Skeleton Man fell in and was washed away.

Then she went back to the longhouse where all her relatives, including her mother and father, had been eaten. All that was left of them were bones. But the rabbit told her what to do.

"Put their bones together," the rabbit said. "Go outside the longhouse and push over that big dead tree. Just before it hits the longhouse call out these words." Then he told her the magic words.

That girl did just as the rabbit said. Just before the tree hit the longhouse she shouted out what the rabbit had told her.

As soon as she did that, all of her relatives were restored with the flesh back on their bones. They jumped out the door, happy and alive.

I was once like the girl in that old story. And not just because I'm a Mohawk, as she was. My parents had vanished without a trace about a year ago. And there was a monster in my story, too. Some people say he was just a man, an evil old man who pretended to be my long-lost uncle after my parents had disappeared, even though he turned out to be the one who kidnapped them and held them prisoner. He meant to do something terrible to all three of us and I am sure he would have if I hadn't escaped. I was even helped by a rabbit, who appeared in my dreams to guide me.

My so-called uncle fooled everyone except me. Social services even sent me to live with him in a spooky old house where he locked me in my room every night. Maybe you remember seeing it on the news, how I escaped from that house and found the place where he was holding my parents captive, how he chased me through the dark until he fell through the old bridge over the gorge. That's where the TV news stories mostly ended. Except for the ominous little mention at the end of each telecast that "the kidnapper's body has not yet been found." It never was.

My father talked about the circle more than usual in the months after it all happened. Not right away, of course. Right after I saved them, we were all so excited and happy and relieved that there was no time to be upset or think too much about it. It wasn't until after we were safe that all three of us started to feel depressed and sad and Dad started talking so much about the circle and I started having bad dreams.

Mrs. Rudder, my school counselor, met with us. Of course, she suggested antidepressants for me. My mother suggested something else to Mrs. Rudder, which made my father laugh. It ended up with the three of us going into family counseling. We could talk about our fears together and not feel foolish.

Together, my dad says, we can overcome anything. Even bad memories like those that were coming back to haunt me after it all supposedly ended when Skeleton Man fell into the gorge.

Gradually, the bad dreams became fewer and then it seemed as if they were gone. I no longer woke up in the middle of the night screaming. It had been months since that happened. But here, at this safe, secure place, where they even have a gatehouse halfway down the mountain where everyone in a car has to stop and be logged in before they can go any farther, the dreams have returned. This last dream has been the worst of all.

"It's over," Mom says. "It was just a dream. He's not coming back."

"I know," I reply, keeping my voice calm.

But I hear another familiar voice saying something else to me. I'm not hearing it with my ears but deep inside my mind.

It's not over, that voice says. *Some dreams are more than just dreams.*

And I nod my head, knowing it to be true.

Some dreams, that rabbit voice continues, *are*

like this one I just sent you. They are messages and warnings.

And even though it sends a shiver down my spine, I understand what this message, this warning, means.

Skeleton Man will return.

4

My So-Called Uncle

"Molly," my mom says, "get dressed, honey. Your father will be here soon and he'll want to use the bathroom."

That's one disadvantage of the suite we're in. Three people and only one bathroom. Being a man, my dad doesn't have to spend much time in there at all. Since he doesn't even have to shave—a lack of male facial hair is just one more advantage of an aboriginal heritage, he jokes—he spends even less time in there than the average man. But there are things that Mom and I each need to do, involving mirrors and brushes and sprays and all that. I'm the kind of girl who wishes it all just came in a bottle you could simply point at yourself and *phhsssshh!* put it all on with one spray. Instant full facial. But lately I am feeling better about the results. So I am now ready to take the time, even though I let out a heavy sigh.

Mom's laying out clothes for my dad to wear to dinner. She likes doing these "girly, wifely things" when we're all together like this because she doesn't usually get to do them every day. She has a master's degree in social work and has done everything from being a drug counselor in a prison to working with unwed mothers. Currently she is the head counselor at a youth camp for juvenile offenders. She is a tough cookie. Of the three of us, Mom seems to have been the least fazed by what we all went through. Then again, she has been faithfully going to a self-defense class for women two nights a week. No way does she plan to ever get kidnapped again without putting up a fight.

I study myself in the mirror. I've got this little crease between my brows that shows up when I'm worried. It's like an anxiety barometer and it's there now. But at least the only face I see in the mirror is my own. In one of the dreams I've started having again, I look into the mirror and see not just my own face but the cold face of Skeleton Man staring over my shoulder.

The one question people kept asking was why did that strange old man do it. There are theories. The most common one has to do with money. He kidnapped my parents because of my father's job with the bank. He was trying to get my father to tell him information that he could use to get a lot of money. It all had to do with wire transfers and offshore accounts in the Cayman Islands. My mom and I were being used as leverage to get my father to do what he wanted. But my father kept stalling him because he knew in his gut what I also believe to be true. As soon as he got what he wanted, my so-called uncle would have killed all three of us.

The investigators found all the stuff they needed to prove that money transfer theory. They found the computers, the phony identification papers, even uniforms he had used to pose as a policeman, a phone company employee, and a security guard.

And they also found evidence that tied him to the disappearance over several previous years of other bank executives in other cities, along with their familes. None of those people were ever seen again. Each of those disappearances had been connected with the loss of large sums of money from their bank. Millions. But the theory, until our family escaped, had always been that those bank people had stolen the money themselves. Before us, there had never been any loose ends. Not even a dead body. I don't like to think about what might have happened to the bodies of those poor innocent people.

Despite all they discovered, the investigators never found anything that told them my so-called uncle's true identity. I don't like to think about that, either. It's bad enough that my dreams and the rabbit had told me that he wasn't a person at all.

"He is Skeleton Man," the rabbit said. "He is a hungry monster just pretending to be human."

A monster. The other theory the state police investigators came up with was that whoever he was, he didn't really do it for the money. He did it for the thrill of controlling people's lives—until it was time for their deaths. He enjoyed playing with us the way a cat toys with a mouse. Monsters—whether they are serial killers or creatures in our old stories—don't see the rest of us as human. They just see us as playthings. Maybe they don't even think of themselves as evil. But I do. I know there's real evil in the world.

But I also know there is good.

"If it wasn't for good," my mother says, "we human beings would have been wiped out a long time ago. Either the monsters would have gotten us or we would have killed each other off with greed and jealousy and anger. So we have to believe in good. We have to look for the good in ourselves."

Sometimes, like that rabbit who turned up in my dreams speaking in a voice like my dad's, there's good outside us, too. There's this old Indian idea about spirit guides. There are forces in the universe that can help us if we prove worthy. They may take the shape of an animal or a bird and appear to us to aid us. That was what the rabbit did for me, just like the rabbit in the old story who helped the girl escape from Skeleton Man.

The thought of that rabbit makes me smile—just as I'm putting on my lipstick. As a result I get some on my teeth. Before I wipe it off with a tissue, I notice how much that red lipstick on my teeth looks like blood. My smile disappears. There's a knot in my stomach again.

I finish wiping off the lipstick and turn toward the bathroom door, where my father has appeared, waiting "patiently" and looking at his wristwatch.

"Hey," he says to my mother, "it's a new record. Molly girl managed to finish before I reached retirement age."

It's one of his corny jokes, but it's so normal that it makes me feel good again and giggle. I pretend to be angry and I elbow him in the side.

"Watch it there, warrior girl," he says with a groan. "The ribs you broke last time still haven't healed."

I love my family. We're together and having fun. There is nothing wrong. Life is good. So why am I so worried? And why does my father also have that little furrow between his brow?

5

By the Lake

Dad has gotten ready even faster than usual, which has left us time for a leisurely stroll along the lake before dinner. Both Mom and I are wearing comfortable shoes, and the paths are all well cared for and easy to walk along. It's so warm today that we don't need heavy coats. The few remaining late-autumn flowers, mums and pansies, are beautiful.

So why does everything around me seem as if it is transparent? Why do I feel as if I am walking on thin ice that might break any minute? Why do I feel as if I am being watched?

Stop it, I tell myself. I'm being an idiot. Is dwelling on the past all I can do?

I need to look at the beauty around me and feel good about being here. I look at an old tree—and notice how one branch is shaped almost like a huge hand about to grab me. I look at the big stones along the trail—and see how one of them has a jagged edge that is almost like a row of hungry teeth.

Quit thinking about dumb things, I command myself. Unfortunately, when you focus on not thinking about something, that is all you can think about. For example, try not to think about a blue elephant.

"Molly, where are you going?"

I hear my dad's voice at the same moment I feel his hand on my elbow, pulling me back onto the path. I'm so distracted that I've almost walked off the trail right over one of the low cliffs and into the lake. It was just absent-mindedness, but I find myself remembering another one of our old Mohawk stories. It's about a monster who lurks underwater and lures unsuspecting people to come closer and closer—like sleepwalkers—until it can grab them and pull them under.

That's a scary tale to most people, but I find it strangely reassuring. It gives me an idea. If I can concentrate on what it would be like if there were a Mohonk Lake monster it may not leave enough room in my mind to worry about . . . something else.

The Monster of Mohonk, I think. A

horrible, terrible old lake creature. I build a picture in my mind of something like a cross between Barney the dinosaur and the snaky Loch Ness monster. In my imagination, it is always hungry, but no one seems to know it is there, even though picnic baskets and pet poodles left by the lake have a habit of disappearing.

When their parents are not around, children come down to the lake, drawn by the monster's hypnotic mind-call. They climb onto his fuzzy purple back. You can almost hear a merry-go-round playing in the background. He carries them out into the center of the lake while he grins back at them with a big, happy, toothless Saturday-morning-kids'-show smile. However (cue the ominous theme music), when they are far enough out he opens his mouth even wider. Now the horrified tots can see that behind his big goofy grin, set farther back in his mouth, are row after row of huge razor-sharp teeth, bigger than those of the shark in *Jaws*.

Ka-chomp, ka-chomp, ka-chomp!

"You're smiling," my mother says, looking at me. "I knew you'd feel more relaxed once we got outside."

It's true—I'm beginning to feel like my old,

imaginative self. The image of that deadly, hungry but goofy lake creature is doing it for me. It fits right in with what my father always said when he told me our old Mohawk stories about monsters: "Molly girl, those monsters were big and dangerous and hungry . . . and stupid. You can use a monster's own weakness against it."

I imagine a girl—a girl who looks like me but a lot younger—who has hidden inside the big old hotel while all the other kids have gone out to play. From behind the curtains of her window she has seen the lake monster scarf down lunch baskets and lure in foolish children. No one believes her when she tells them what she has seen. So she knows it is up to her. Her big brother has brought a bag of illegal fireworks with him on their vacation. She connects them all together with a long fuse, then she goes down to the deceptively peaceful lake with all those firecrackers in a picnic basket. She notices bubbles rising to the surface about fifty feet out and she nods to herself.

Quickly she lights the long fuse, puts down the basket, and calls out in a loud voice, "Oops, I have forgotten something and now I have to run back to my room. But all of this delicious food will be safe here beside the lake, where nothing big and purple and hungry and stupid can get it."

Then she turns and runs as fast as she can.

She has taken only a few steps before she hears the slosh of water and a loud gulp. She turns back to look and sees nothing but ripples and a few bubbles moving away from shore.

Wha-boomp! There is a big underwater explosion. A little geyser shoots up from the center of the lake, followed by pieces of purple monster flesh.

I keep refining that story in my mind as we reach the steps that lead up into the main building. Maybe after the monster is destroyed that little girl does something magical. Maybe she sings a song or throws some sweetgrass into the water, then all of the kids that were eaten by the monster come bobbing up to the surface, alive and well, although coated with monster slime—along with a hundred happy, yappy poodles. They swim back to the shore, where their bewildered, overjoyed parents—and dog owners—are waiting for them.

I turn at the top of the steps to look at the lake and the cliff that rises above it. Then I look back at the huge old building itself, at its dark old wood and stone. I could wander the long, echoey hallways of this place for days and never see it all. There aren't just big meeting rooms and places where concerts and shows take place; there are also creaky stairways, balconies, and closed doors that probably lead down into basement rooms where no one goes. Mohonk Mountain House is spooky. In fact, I'd be surprised if it wasn't haunted by at least a ghost or three. But the thought of ghosts doesn't scare me. Like the imaginary lake monster whose story I've been creating, spectral beings are a better alternative than the reality of what my parents and I actually survived. That was a real horror story—too real.

Just like that, with one careless thought, my whole reassuring scary fantasy vanishes as quickly and completely as a soap bubble broken by the breeze. The knot in my stomach grabs hold once more. Everything around me that had just seemed old and safely quaint has suddenly become ominous. I really am as afraid as a little kid left alone in a haunted house. There are lots of other people around me, people here for my dad's conference, and others who've come to eat in the famous dining room or take part in the other programs that are always going on here—like the Adirondack musicians named Quickstep who'll be playing in the Lake Room tomorrow night.

But now I am feeling totally alone in this crowd. I don't want to look at any faces for fear that one of those strangers might look familiar, that I might see the cold, calculating eyes of Skeleton Man staring at me. In fact, I feel right now as if someone is watching me from behind, from just above me. But I don't allow myself to turn and look up toward the landing. I push through the crowd, trying not to sob, trying to catch my breath.

There is one part of the old Mohawk story of Skeleton Man that I usually leave out, even though it was always in the version my father told me. It's the part that is freaking me out right now. It's the part where, after the monster seems safely gone and everyone has been rescued, that rabbit comes back and whispers something in the little girl's ear. You may already have guessed what it is.

"The monster is not really dead. Skeleton Man will come back again."

By the time I catch up to my parents, who had gotten only a little ahead of me, I've regained my composure. I even manage to paint a smile on my face before I get to them, but I'm no longer feeling happy as we walk along the hall to the main dining room. And I can still feel eyes watching my back.

6

Dark Corridors

Gormenghast. That is the title of a trilogy of old fantasy novels I heard about when they were made into a TV miniseries a few years ago. It's about this ancient castle that is so large it stretches for miles, with dark corridors and hidden rooms and strange characters. There's all kinds of murder and intrigue in the story.

"This looks like Gormenghast" was my first thought when we drove around the corner in our car and I saw where we were staying. Admittedly, it wasn't miles long, but it was huge and it looked even bigger, being way up on top of this mountain.

"Heeeere's Johnny," my father said, leering at my mother as we walked down the corridor toward the registration desk.

"Stop that," my mother said, trying not to laugh.

"All work and no play makes Jack a dull

boy," my father replied in a mock creepy voice.

My mom punched him in the arm.

"Ouch," he said, pretending to be hurt.

"Next time it's the baseball bat," Mom answered.

I love it when my parents do that kind of thing. My dad likes to quote lines from scary movies and pretend to be the monster in them. Right then he was imitating Jack Nicholson in that movie *The Shining*, where this guy and his wife and little son go all alone to an old resort hotel way up in the mountains because he is the winter caretaker, but he gets driven crazy by the ghosts there and tries to kill his family.

For a while, after Skeleton Man, my parents stopped playing that game. I think someone had advised them to soft-pedal stuff like that around me because it might upset their poor traumatized daughter in her delicate condition. Actually, it was more upsetting to me to have them walking around on eggshells, trying not to say the wrong thing or do anything that might set me off. It made me feel fragile, like a piece of antique china locked up in a cupboard.

I finally realized I had to do something. I knocked on the door of their room one night. I just knew they were up and talking about me.

Sure enough, when they told me to come on in, I could hear that little hesitation in their voices that made me certain they'd been talking about poor Molly.

I sat down on the edge of the bed, then leaned over and put my head on my father's shoulder.

"Daddy," I said, "tell me a story."

"I don't know," my father said. My mom bit her lip.

I sat up and looked first at him and then at Mom.

"Listen," I said, "I'm still Molly. Remember me? I need to hear a story. And make it a scary one, okay?"

I guess the tone of my voice must have been a little stronger than I intended because both my parents raised their eyebrows. Then my mother laughed.

"She's baa-aack," my father said. And then he told me a story that was so scary I asked my parents if I could sleep with them that night. All three of us fell asleep with a smile on our face.

The thing about scary stories, you see, is that they're reassuring. At least they are for me. Like I said before, life really is dangerous. There truly are things for people to be afraid of—if not giant cannibals in the forest, then other people who can be just as dangerous. The stories have always helped me deal with my fears. Remember, the scariest monster is the one you don't see. After that big mechanical shark in *Jaws* finally comes to the surface and starts chomping on the boat, it is nowhere near as terrifying as it was at the start of the movie, when you just heard that music and then saw a swirl of blood and one or two leftover body parts sinking to the bottom. So the stories help me see my fears and then deal with them. Once Dad started telling stories again, we really did get back to normal.

Coming to this conference with my parents is yet another way of their letting me know they think I'm ready to deal with the outside world—or at least the microcosm that is Mohonk. This huge resort hotel has more than seven hundred employees. Some of them live in New Paltz and the other little communities around Mohonk, but a lot of them stay right here on the premises in the dormitory for workers.

I can understand why. The main road that leads up to the Mohonk Mountain House is winding and long. I can't imagine what it was like building it. In some spots the road is narrow and right next to the edge of the cliffs, which have long drop-offs. It must take a lot of maintenance to keep the road open in winter or to repair it when there are rock slides. I saw some big machines—a bulldozer, a front-end loader, and a dump truck—parked in a pull-off area where the road started winding around after we passed the gatehouse.

"How'd you like to drive that baby?" my dad said to me, pointing at the bulldozer with his chin as we slowly passed it.

"I'd love it," I said.

I wasn't kidding. Dad operated machinery like that during the summers when he was working his way through college. He's never lost his love for those things and keeps little yellow model construction vehicles of all kinds on a shelf by his desk. He's remained friends with some of the men he worked with back then and visits them now and then on their jobs. I must have inherited that "knock things down, build things up" gene, as my mom calls it, from my father.

I've gone along with him on some of those jaunts. It is usually a real hands-on visit, because Dad always has to climb up into the cab of whatever new behemoth they've got and try the controls. I don't know how many times I've sat on his lap, my own yellow hardhat on my head, with my hands on his as he drove a front-end loader or dozer, or operated a crane. Since I've gotten older, I've even been allowed to work the controls myself at times. Nowadays there are women on some sites operating those big machines.

On the drive up here I didn't notice anyone using the bulldozer or loader. They probably wouldn't have been left unguarded like that if they hadn't been on this side of the gatehouse, secure. The gatehouse marks the start of the private Mohonk road. It's the only official way in. This main road ends at a loop, with the Mountain House at the far end of it. There's a smaller, secondary road called Mossy Brook Road that swings off that loop, but it is so little it makes the narrow main road look like a superhighway.

Everyone who comes up to the Mountain House has to check in at the Mohonk Mountain House gate just like we did our first day. You have to be an employee with ID, or your name has to be on the guest list, or you have to pay a fee to come up for the day or to get lunch or dinner. You have to either park your car in a big lot near the gatehouse and take the shuttle bus up or drive your car the remaining two miles to where the valets park it for you.

That is one reason why my dad's convention is being held here, because it is so organized and safe and secure. It is what they call a "controlled environment."

But lots of events do take place here. Dad's conference isn't the only thing going on. At Mohonk this weekend they are also celebrating the Day of the Dead, which is a Mexican festival, along with Halloween. Halloween, as every kid knows, is on October 31. Its name comes, as a lot of kids *don't* know, from the eve of All Hallows, a time to celebrate all the Christian saints. (Forgive me, but you are now dealing with Molly the information junkie, who you should never ever dare to take on in a game of Trivial Pursuit.)

The Day of the Dead is actually the two days right after Halloween, November 1 and 2. It is an old indigenous celebration. The Aztecs celebrated it around the end of what we call the month of July. It was presided over by Mictecacihuatl, the "Lady of the Dead," who was a powerful, benevolent being who loved little children and even acted as their protector, a sort of messenger from the ancestors, who were always watching over their descendants. But the priests who arrived with the Spanish conquistadors didn't appreciate that the local people followed the old ways. They wanted them to honor just the Christian saints. They tried to wipe out the holiday, but the Indians wouldn't give it up. So the Spanish moved it to the beginning of November to coincide with El Día de Todos Santos, the Day of All Saints or All Saints' Day, as well as All Souls' Day.

The Day of the Dead is huge in Mexico, where life and death are seen in a different way than they are in most of the United States. People go to cemeteries to honor their dead relatives. There are fireworks and people dress up in devil masks and costumes to look like skeletons. They even give kids candy shaped like little skulls. Because there are so many Mexican Americans in the United States, it has been popular in the American Southwest, too. It's a new idea having a Day of the Dead here at the hotel, almost two thousand miles from Mexico. The poster I read about it says that it is Mohonk Mountain House's way of "continuing to celebrate the multicultural tapestry that is the United States today." Whatever.

Some people would say that my parents were either cruel or crazy to take a kid who'd experienced the kind of trauma I did to a place where they were celebrating not just Halloween but also the Day of the Dead. Not just one event focusing on ghosts and death but two. Practically child abuse. But I think it's great. My parents always told me that you have to face your fears. If you turn away from them, they can just sneak up and grab you from behind. The fact that my parents would actually take me to something like this after all we went through with Skeleton Man really shows how much they believe I have gotten back to normal.

Normal, though, doesn't necessarily mean safe.

Like right now.

They are showing a movie tonight here at the hotel, right after the music is done. I've been feeling antsy all day, actually ever since dinner last night. I guess I need to get out of the room. It's a full hour till the concert starts, so I've decided to poke around the hotel. Dad has an evening meeting and won't be able to go to the concert, although he'll join us in time for the film.

Mom has told me she'll meet me at the concert. Rather than head straight there, I decided to go upstairs and explore the wing I haven't seen yet. So here I am walking this long dark corridor alone.

There's this sound that your feet make on a wooden floor when no one else is walking on it but you, like the floor is talking to you in a different language. You don't know how to speak that language, but you can comprehend it the same way you understand the growling of a big animal that's out there just beyond the light of your fire.

Kuhh-reeeaak. Kuhh-reeeaak.

Walking slower just makes it worse. This hallway seems to go on forever. I try walking faster. I'm humming "A Little Bit of Luck" under my breath to the beat of my footsteps, but not the whole song, because I don't know it. Just this one refrain, which shows how nervous I am making myself.

With a little bit,
with a little bit,

with a little bit of luck
I won't get caught.

Caught by what? This is dumb. I stop humming. Immediately I start to notice that the sound of my footsteps is getting louder. Each footfall seems to be echoing. Am I hearing someone else's feet hitting just half a step after mine? I stop and listen, but I don't hear anything. I pretend to take a step, then whirl around to look behind me. There's nothing there but the empty hall and the old black-and-white photos hanging along the walls. Not even a shadow. Every door is closed. Nothing to be afraid of.

But I start running anyway. Sometimes seeing nothing is just as ominous as seeing something. I don't know if that sounds crazy, but right now it makes sense to me. I find a stairway and I thud down it, and all of a sudden I'm not alone at all. Just half a flight below me I see people walking along, talking and acting normal. One or two of them are turning to look up at the wild-eyed teenager descending the stairs like a deer stampeding down a slope away from a mountain lion.

"Take it easy, honey," I hear a woman say.

She's got hold of my arm—not so hard that it hurts, but firm enough to have stopped my headlong progress. It takes me a second to realize that she's just saved me from running into her and sending both of us rolling down the stairs. She must be a maid, because she is wearing one of the hotel's uniforms. The towels she dropped when she grabbed me are at her feet. She is also holding a big red potted chrysanthemum in her other arm. Its heady smell is all around us.

"I'm sorry," I say. "I just . . ." Just what? I don't know.

"S'all right, honey," the woman says. She has some kind of accent, maybe Central American. She looks up at me as she says this, because she is not at all tall, no more than five feet, but she looks compact and strong. Her face is even a little browner than my dad's and I find myself wondering how much Indian blood she has. Her ID tag tells me her name is Corazón.

"You all right?" she says. Her voice is soft, confidential.

I nod.

She lets go of my arm to set the chrysanthemum down on the landing. Then she picks up the towels, places them on a little seat built into the stairwell behind her, and straightens out my sweater, which has gotten twisted around. Her touch is as reassuring as my mom's.

"Thanks," I say.

Corazón smiles. She looks at my face closely and then nods in recognition. "Indio," she says. It's not a question.

"I'm Mohawk."

Corazón smiles at me again, one of those smiles that just lights up a face. She puts her right hand on her heart.

"Mayan," she says.

I'm not sure when we sat down, but we're sitting together now, as if we were old friends. I hope I'm not getting her into trouble because she's supposed to be working, but I'm really glad that she's here with me. I look over at the towels she was carrying.

"S'all right," Corazón says again. "My shift is just over. I take these down, drop them off, go home. It is my time now."

I'm feeling a lot saner now. Sane enough to be embarrassed. "I'm sorry," I say. "I don't know what made me do that."

Corazón leans over toward me and looks into my eyes. Her own eyes are dark, just like mine. Her face is also just as smooth and unlined as mine, but I'm sure she is older than me. Not as old as my mom, but she has to be at least twenty.

"This place," she says. She doesn't say it as if she is afraid or unhappy about being here. It's more like she is just making an observation. "Sometimes when I walk up there, I think I am not alone. You maybe felt like somebody was looking at you?"

"That's it," I say. "That's exactly it."

"*Los muertos*," Corazón says. "The dead are watching."

7

Down the Hallway

Corazón is waving at me from the doorway, not with her whole hand but with her fingers in a fluttery gesture that makes me think of a butterfly. She's smiling as she waves and then she touches her heart. I smile back and tap my own chest with the fingers of my right hand. I feel such a connection to her.

Part of it is her being Indian, like me. Just from our short talk, too, I can tell that she understands things I can't talk to a lot of people about. Things that some people would call being foolish or superstitious. Things like being guided by your dreams.

"My great-great-grandfather," she had told me in a soft, sure voice that had only a little bit of a Spanish accent. "His name was Chan K'in. That means 'Little Sun' or 'Little Prophet.' He was over 130 years old when he passed away a few years ago. We little ones would sit at his feet around the fire at night and he would tell stories. Then every morning he would ask us what we had dreamed about. He would listen closely to our dreams and help us understand the messages those dreams brought to us. He taught me how to interpret dream messages."

So I told her about the rabbit and about Skeleton Man. Just the short version. But it still took twenty minutes.

When I finished my story, Corazón shivered as if she had just felt a cold breeze. Then she reached out one hand and tapped it lightly on the wood bench where we were sitting. I understood that gesture. You knock on wood when you think something bad may be about to happen. It's a way of summoning good to come and protect you. She was silent for a while before she spoke again.

"I think my great-great-grandfather might have said your rabbit was speaking with an ancestor's voice. He was watching over you in the same way that our Lady of the Dead always watches out for our children. Do you know about the one the Azteca call Mictecacihuatl?"

"A little," I replied. That brought a smile to Corazón's face.

"I think you have *mucho fortuna*," she said. "Much fortune."

"I think so too," I replied.

I looked at my watch. I had that feeling you get when a story has just ended and you find yourself back in the "real" world again, and you wonder how much time has passed. This time it was more than I'd realized.

"Oh my gosh," I said. "It's almost time for the concert. I have to meet my mom."

Corazón picked up her towels, put them under one arm, and stood. "Come," she said, holding out her hand to me. "I know the quickest way to get there."

"What a lovely young woman," Mom says as Corazón disappears around the corner. "It was very nice of her to help you find your way here after you got turned around. This is a big place and those long hallways can be confusing."

More than just confusing, I think. But I am not going to mention to Mom how freaked out I was before I ran into Corazón . . . or how I almost ran over her.

Mom had asked Corazón if she could stay and listen to the music with us, but Corazón shook her head and said something in Spanish that I didn't catch. But my mother, who speaks not just Mohawk and English—like my dad and me—but also three or four other languages, nodded and answered something back to her in Spanish that made Corazón put her hand over her mouth and giggle.

I wait until Corazón is out of sight and turn to my mom.

"What did she say?" I demand. Typical Molly. I always have to know everything that is going on.

"Just a proverb, honey. I'll tell you later. The music's about to start. I think you're going to like this."

By the time the evening concert is over, an hour later, I'm in total agreement with my mother. In fact, I didn't just like it, I loved it. I even danced with my mom to a couple of the square dance tunes they played. Contrary to what she and Dad had told me, there were *not* lots of kids my age at the dance. But that was okay. Also, one member of Quickstep was a cute guy who probably wasn't much older than me. He looked shy, but I am sure he smiled at me once or twice. It made me feel like he was playing just for me. He had a very cool name, too—Cedar, just like the tree.

"I hope we can see that group again sometime," I say to Mom as we walk toward the movie. I am totally at ease now and there is nothing at all scary about the corridor that was so creepy when I was walking it on my own.

"Did you see that boy who was playing the fiddle?" she says.

"Mom!" I hate it when she seems to read my mind like this. I stop and stare at her. "I was talking about the group, not just that one guy. What do you mean?"

"I just meant," she says, a little smile on her lips, "that he seemed very talented, even though he was so young."

"Oh," I say, my face reddening. "Yes, I guess so."

Then I smile like my mom is smiling. Maybe everything is going to be all right after all. We meet up with my dad and I manage to keep thinking that way all through the movie. But as we are walking back, I find myself a few steps behind my parents. I stop to look at one of the old photos on the wall, and suddenly I get that feeling again. I'm being watched. I spin around to look down the hall behind me. For just a second I think I see someone, a tall, thin person with a pale face fading back into a

doorway. I take one step in that direction, then another.

"Molly."

My mom's voice brings me out of my trance. I turn around and realize that I have walked back the whole length of the hall. My hand is holding the knob of the door through which I thought I saw that tall, pale shape disappear.

I jerk my hand back like it's been burned. I don't want to open this door. A shiver goes down my spine as I turn and head back toward my mother, who's holding out her hand to me, a questioning look on her face. I force myself to walk to her, even though I want to run. I manage to force a smile back onto my face.

There's nothing wrong, I tell myself.

But the knot in my stomach is as hard as a fist. Was my imagination going crazy on me or had I really seen someone disappear through that door? I am afraid to think that I know the answer—and who might be waiting on the other side.

8

The Lookout

The next morning it is sunny when I wake up. At first that seems strange, because I feel as if I was just in a very dark, unpleasant place, and this room is the opposite of that. I feel as if there are cobwebs on my face, and I wipe my eyes. I know I was having a bad dream, but this time I can't quite remember what it was. Or maybe I just don't want to remember.

I get up and let the sunshine touch my face. A little breeze is coming through the open window. There's still that taste in the air that you get in fall when the light outside is so clear that it seems to vibrate and it is as warm as some summer days. I can tell it's a fragile warmth. It might blow away as quickly as the seeds on a dandelion, but it makes me want to go outside and walk. I need to do something like stroll through a garden and this is the best place to do that.

"I'm going for a walk," I say, looking into my parents' room after getting ready.

"Want me to come along?" my mom asks.

There's a breakfast tray with coffee and juice and pastries in front of her and my father. I know she's not ready yet to go out. She'd probably like to have some time alone with Dad, who doesn't have to leave for his next seminar for another two hours. But she's ready to come with me if I need company. The thought of the two of them sitting together and having breakfast makes me feel warm and secure. It's like sunshine on my face.

"It's okay," I say. "I'd just like to walk by myself and check out the summerhouses. I am going to try to sit in every single one."

That makes my dad laugh. He knows I'll try to do it, even though there are over a hundred summerhouses here at Mohonk. They even sell a little booklet in the gift shop called *The Summerhouses of Mohonk.* They aren't like gazebos, which are intricate and planned. The summerhouses of Mohonk are rustic. Some are nothing more than a bench with a roof, and every one is different. A lot of them are made of dark, old, twisting cedar logs with the bark still on them. They're like grandparents, just waiting for you to climb up onto their laps.

And that's what I do. I sit in each one that I find, lean back, feel how it is to be there, look out at the view it commands, give a contented sigh, and then head to the next one.

Every single summerhouse is placed so it has a different scenic view. I said there were over a hundred, but no one knows for sure how many there are. The earliest inventory was done in 1917 when they listed 155 summerhouses. Nowadays they claim there are 125. Most have a brass tag with a four-digit number that is entered into the Mohonk computer base. But there may still be forgotten ones tucked off in the woods. Some of them are way down winding paths and others are perched up on the edges of cliffs, with wooden bridges and stairs leading to them. The one on Sentinel Rock overlooks the lake and the whole Mountain House. The best ones, though, as far as I'm concerned, overlook the flower gardens. Although most of the flowers are gone now, you can see how beautiful this place must be when they are in bloom.

"House number twenty-eight," I say to myself.

The sun is still shining in my face as I settle

down on the cedar bench. A bent wood roof with rough shingles hangs over it, covered by a vine of some kind that has been trained over the top. At its base that vine is as thick as my waist, and I wonder how old it is. My eyes follow it as it climbs from the ground toward the roof, then something in the distance catches my eye.

I'm looking out at one of the wooded ridges that rise above the gardens. It is at least two hundred yards away and a hundred feet higher in elevation than me. There's another summerhouse there, one that I hadn't noticed before. Even with the leaves off the trees, it is hard to see it, tucked away up there on the lookout. But it's not the summerhouse that has caught my eye—rather, a flash of light from inside it. It's the kind of flash of light when the sun hits a mirror or something made of glass.

I raise up my hand to shade my eyes. Another flash of light comes from inside that summerhouse on the highest slope. And even though it is so far away, I am certain about what I'm seeing. It's a pair of binoculars and they are pointing right at me. I can just barely make out the pale head and gloved hands of the person holding them. That person is wearing a hat, and he's so far away I can't really see his face, but something tells me that it's a man. While I'm staring, those binoculars are slowly pulled back. All I can see now is the shadowy opening of the summerhouse.

I wait. For some reason, my heart is thumping in my chest, even though there's no reason to get upset about somebody with binoculars. People carry them around here all the time. It's the season when hawks migrate. Just yesterday there was a whole gaggle of bird-watchers on the ridge, all staring up through their spotting scopes and binoculars at a huge flock of broad-winged hawks sweeping by, following the Shawangunk Ridge toward the south.

Staring up. That's it. You don't look down to see hawks, you look up into the sky. There's still no motion from the summerhouse on the ridge. The way the trees grow around it I can see only the front from where I'm sitting. I have to go there. Half of my brain says I'm being foolish, that there's nothing to be afraid of. The other half says I'm being foolhardy. Why am I taking the path that leads up to that lookout? How do I know there's not something dangerous up there just waiting for me?

I'm breathing hard by the time I reach the

summerhouse on the ridge. I can see now that it is balanced right on top of a huge, flat boulder. There's no one here. I look around. No sign of anyone on the gravel path leading down in either direction. Was I just imagining that I saw someone?

I sit down on the bench and look down. There's a perfect view of not just the garden but also the Mountain House itself. I spot the summerhouse where I had been sitting. I have to lean out and to the right to get a clear view of it. As I do so, I put my hand on the bench. My palm finds something small and round, something that I hadn't noticed when I sat down. When I see what it is, a chill shivers down my back and I almost drop what I'm holding—a small, perfectly molded white candy skull.

9

Skulls

I still have the candy skull in my hand. But now I'm feeling like a jerk. I sprinted all the way back to the Mountain House in a panic, thumped up the steps, burst through the door of the Lake Lounge and what did I see? The tables are awash with marigolds and chrysanthemums. And in the midst of those flowers are bowls half-filled with candy skulls just like mine. The candy skulls are just part of the whole Day of the Dead theme. Some of them look like human skulls and some are like the skulls of animals. Boys and girls are wandering around with their parents, candy skulls in their hands—or their mouths. Some kid was probably walking on that path, sat down in the summerhouse, and just left the skull up there by accident. Nothing sinister. Just kids and candy.

The one I have in my hand has gotten

sticky from the sweat in my palm. It's starting to dissolve, just like the panic that had gripped me so hard that I felt as if I had been hit in the stomach.

Get a grip, girl, I tell myself. I pick up a paper napkin, wrap my no longer ominous piece of candy in it, and drop it into a wastebasket. Then I wipe my hand clean. I won't mention this to my parents. I'll just let them think I had a great walk. No attack of absolute gut-wrenching terror. It was just a carefree afternoon for me, sitting in one summerhouse after another, enjoying the quiet beauty and feeling that all was right with the world.

I head back to my room, say hi to my parents, and then slump into the chair by the window and pick up my book for a bit of leisurely reading. Only I can't concentrate on anything. I can't shake this eerie feeling that something just isn't right.

No. Everything is fine. Just fine.

"Time for dinner, honey," Mom announces after a while. "Are you ready?"

My parents and I get a table near the windows in the big semi-circular dining room with the high ceiling and wooden beams. Our table would normally be a great place to sit because you can look way out over the valleys and see the far-off lights of houses and the shadowy hills in the twilight. But this evening all I can see is mist. I can't even see the trees and bushes on the lawn right below. I'm feeling closed in, trapped. I wish I could see through that mist, and see if anything was out there. Then I start thinking about what I might see, what I don't want to see. I squirm in my seat.

"Molly," Dad says, "are you okay?"

He and Mom are looking right at me. I almost give them one of those "Oh, I'm fine" replies. I don't want to worry them needlessly, after everything we've gone through. But my mouth reacts before my brain can stop it.

"No," I say. "I'm not." For some reason, that actually makes me feel a little better.

"Why, honey?" Mom asks. But something about the way she asks it tells me that she already has a good idea.

"I feel," I say, balling my napkin up between my palms, "like I'm being watched by . . . somebody."

I wait for them to reassure me, to tell me I am being foolish. But they don't. Instead, my mother and father exchange a long look, and finally my father nods.

"I know," Dad says. "I've been feeling the same way. There's something not quite right lately. I keep telling myself that I'm being foolish, but I still have bad dreams about what happened to us. I don't see . . . him . . . in my dreams, but I can feel him watching us. Then, the next thing I know, my hands are tied and you and Mom are in danger and I can't get free to save you."

My mouth drops open and I stare at my father. I've never thought about how he and Mom were affected by what happened to us. All I've been able to think about are my own feelings. But they were in just as much danger as I was. And my dad, who I used to think was big and strong and smart enough to defeat any monster in the world, had been helpless.

"They never found his body," I say. I'm amazed at how calm and logical my voice sounds.

"I know," Dad replies.

"Why would he come after us?"

My mom is the one who answers that. "Because we got away," she says. "Because we got away."

"I feel," I say, pausing for a moment and then just saying it, "I feel as if he's here somewhere. Am I crazy?"

I look at my parents closely. I think what I really want is for them to tell me there is nothing to fear, that we are totally safe now and forever. But that is not what they do.

"You're not crazy," Mom says.

"No, you are not," Dad agrees, his voice slow and careful. "I feel as if . . . he . . . is here, too."

"Sk . . . Sk . . . ," I say, trying to speak the name that none of us have wanted to ever hear again.

"Skeleton Man," Mom says.

10

Walking the Field

One thing that scary movies never really focus on is all the times when nothing happens. They make it seem as if one frightening thing always happens right after another without any letup. But life isn't like that. Sometimes, for long stretches of time, nothing at all happens. You just find yourself waiting, and waiting, and not really knowing what is going to happen or when.

And that is how it has been for the rest of the day, after Mom and Dad and I had our conversation about Skeleton Man. We talked it over and came to what we thought were good decisions.

"Should we call the police?" I asked.

"No, I don't think so," Mom said.

Dad nodded. "All we have are suspicions, Molly girl. You *think* you saw something. And Mom and I both have that kind of sixth-sense tingle at the back of our neck. The kind of feeling which my gramma said meant something was looking your way that you didn't want to meet. And you've got your dreams. But it doesn't mean as much as a hill of beans to the authorities. We'd have to have some solid evidence. Something you could sink your teeth into."

"More than a candy skull?" I said.

It wasn't that funny, but I giggled as I said it and then both Dad and Mom were laughing. It released the tension we were all sensing and made us feel so much better. We could still laugh and be together. Everything could still turn out all right.

We came up with sort of a plan. A big part of it was to all be on our guard. I would stay close to either Mom or Dad the rest of the time we were here. We wouldn't leave Mohonk until the conference was over, because we couldn't be sure that we really were in danger. No foolish risks, though. No shopping trip down to New Paltz. No more of my solo hikes along the trails or down darkened corridors.

But we wouldn't act like timid little mice who suspect they are being stalked by a cat. If we just cut and ran every time we got worried, our lives wouldn't belong to us anymore. We'd never be at peace if all we did was try to escape. And besides, we would be here only two more days. Not only that, this was such a special, beautiful place. If we let our fear of something that might or might not happen prevent us from enjoying it, then Skeleton Man really would have won.

One thing that is different now is that I have a cell phone. After all that happened, when it was over, Dad gave me one to keep with me wherever I go.

"Indian telepathy is okay," he said, "but this way I can hear your voice when you need to talk to me."

We both chuckled about that reference to my sixth sense. In the old, old days, some of our elders say, people could really communicate with each other mind-to-mind. A cell phone is a pretty good substitute for that legendary kind of communication.

Having my little phone in my pocket all the time has made me feel more secure. Mom has one, too. So we can make an emergency call to one another or to the authorities at any time. And that is part of our plan, too. If anyone sees or experiences anything out of the ordinary, anything threatening, we can just flip out our phone, hit the button, and communicate. If we learn something tangible, if we really do see Skeleton Man, then we can call the police.

There is another side to our plan. If we don't act all spooked and if Skeleton Man is really here, really watching us, maybe he'll make some kind of mistake. He has underestimated us before, and he might again. So we planned to do fun things—especially things where there would be a lot of people around, like concerts or the afternoon tea, or the Day of the Dead party planned for the next night.

The rest of that evening after dinner the three of us felt so much better, because we had a plan, that the time just whizzed by. We went to bed, and even though we had concluded there was a real chance that our lives were in danger, we had a good night's sleep. We got up and ate breakfast. Dad went to his meetings while Mom and I took a walk together. Then we sat around and read. I did my reading in the window seat where I could look out at the lake and the cliffs across the way and I finished *Briar Rose*. Mom tried to get through the latest historical novel she was reading, but every time I looked up she would either just be staring off into space or be looking over at me. She didn't really relax until we met Dad for lunch.

"Quiet morning, girls?" he asked.

"Unh-huh," I said.

Mom just nodded, and she squeezed Dad's hand under the table most of the time we were eating. Then Mom and I went to an early afternoon chamber music concert in the Lake Lounge.

To the outside world, we've been acting as if we don't have a care in the world, but it's just an act. If we are being watched, we don't want to make it look like we're suspicious.

And now it is time for us to do part of what we'd planned. Mom pulls out the *Historical Features of the Mountain House* booklet that we just bought at the gift shop.

"Well, we have a couple of hours before afternoon tea. Shall we do that self-guided tour, honey?" she asks.

She sounds like she is reading bad dialogue from a second-rate movie. That is one problem with having made a plan. Spontaneity is hard to fake. And my response to her, despite myself, is just as bright and stiff.

"Sure, Mom, that sounds like a great idea."

We take a look at the map inside the booklet. We actually have already spent time studying it. It shows the five huge interconnected wings that make up the Mountain House. Rock Building, Stone Building, Central Building, Grove Building, and the Kitchen and Dining Room Building.

"Oh," Mom says, with the inflection of a bad high school understudy trying to remember her lines now that the lead actress has come down with the flu, "there's our friend. *¿Cómo está usted?*"

"*Bien, gracias,*" Corazón answers. Thankfully, her voice is not at all strained. It helps Mom and me to relax. What helps even more is when, as she gives each of us a hug, she whispers, "Don't worry" in our ears.

Our accidental meeting is no accident. After dinner we had found Corazón and asked her to help us. So she's arranged to have this afternoon off to walk the corridors with us. Corazón, who has worked here for almost a year, is going to point out things that most tourists would not care about or need to know.

The three of us just look like friends strolling along, talking and laughing. But inside, Mom and I are not just being tourists. We're doing what my dad used to do when he was a star lacrosse player. Before each match he would walk the field to familiarize himself with every inch of the place where the game would be played.

And as we do this, as Corazón whispers things to us like where keys are kept and what the hidden ways are in this huge old maze of a place, that feeling from yesterday comes back again. It's like walking into a darkened room, right into a spiderweb that you don't see until it brushes across your face and sticks there.

11

Snow

We've made it through the day. Dad and Mom and I are sitting at our favorite table by the window. Nothing strange has happened except for the snow. A freak storm has swept in from the west and is dumping more snow than I have ever seen in October. From what the forecasters say, it is falling mostly here in the mountains. Down in the valley below, there is hardly any snow at all, and in some cases there is just cold rain.

Snow. All kinds of thoughts are going through my head. Memories of making snowballs, and snow angels and snowmen, and forts. Up on the Rez, snow always means it is time to lay down boards on the back lawn and turn on the hose to make an instant hockey rink. Even though I didn't grow up on the Rez, Dad has made sure I've always had my own skates, and I can swing a stick as well as any boy. When we go up there in the winter, I have my skates and pads, ready to take on my cousins in one of our knock-'em-down, drag-'em-out pick-up games. Lots of scoring and bloody noses. I'm good enough so that I am usually one of the first three or four picked for a side. There's such a feeling of freedom when you can just glide over the ice as if you are flying—and then bodycheck someone so that he flies head over heels into one of the snowdrifts around the rink and steal the puck from him.

There are also Mohawk stories involving snow. Terrible giants sometimes show up in the stories my dad tells. Their skins and their hearts are made of ice and they have no human feelings, just a hunger that can never be satisfied.

The snow swirls across the window. This is ice-giant weather for sure. The waiter stops by our table.

"I know you folks said you weren't planning on going anywhere," he says, "but I thought I should let you know that this storm has gotten pretty bad." He looks out the window and shakes his head. "We don't get anything like this in the Dominican Republic. Anyhow, they've closed the road down the mountain. Nobody will be getting out of here tonight."

Nobody will be getting out of here. Those few innocent words send a chill down my back.

While we wait for our food to come, we don't talk. Instead, Dad and Mom and I just look out the window at the swirling patterns of snow. It is hard to see any shapes beyond the branches of the nearest trees. They still have autumn leaves and the snow is making their branches bend dangerously low to the ground, strained to the point of breaking. Weather like this knocks down not just branches but also power lines and phone lines and then you are cut off from the outside world. I don't like the thought of that.

There could be almost anything out there hidden by that snow. There could be a huge hairy elephant, just like the one in that story by Rafe Martin called *Will's Mammoth*. That used to be my favorite picture book when I was little. Or there could be a whole army of ice giants creeping up on us through the howling storm. I try to imagine them out there, those huge monsters from the old tales. Thinking of mammoths and ice giants is a lot safer than thinking about the one real monster that I escaped from. Imaginary monsters are nowhere near as scary. And the stories always end with you sitting safe and warm at home or around the fire in the longhouse.

But my thoughts won't stay in that safe, fanciful place. Anything could be hidden by that snow. Anything.

12

Masks

The Day of the Dead party is being held in the Lake Lounge tonight. We have decided to be totally minimalist in what we're wearing. No full-face masks hide our features. Just those little Lone Ranger masks. No weird alien outfits with extra limbs. We want to be able to see and recognize one another when we are in the crowd of people. Dad is dressed as a Mohawk high-steel construction worker. That was easy for him. He had thought ahead when he was packing and brought along his old work clothes, from his boots and coveralls to the hardhat with an eagle painted on it. He even has a big spanner wrench stuck in his belt.

Mom and I aren't really wearing costumes. We never use the word *costume* to describe traditional clothing. What we have on is just that, the traditional buckskin dresses with beautiful beadwork that we wear to powwows. We hear appreciative remarks from people as we sweep by. The only risk is that someone will think Mom and I are supposed to be dressed as Pocahontas and her mother. No way. I am Molly Brant, warrior woman. And Mom is dressed as Jigonsaseh, the woman who helped the Peacemaker and Hiawatha found the great Iroquois League of Peace by being the first person to speak in favor of their idea.

The clothing we're wearing is not just beautiful. It is also comfortable and practical, too. You can run in a buckskin dress. It doesn't hold you back and restrict you like long dresses with petticoats and tight cinched-in waists. I see some of the girls going down the hall dressed in Cinderella costumes. If they got knocked over, it would be as hard for them to get up as it is for a turtle to get off its back.

Corazón is going to be here at the party, working. I close my eyes to imagine how she might look in traditional garb and I suddenly see her in my mind's eye. She's wearing a calf-length white dress decorated with beautiful embroidery in all the colors of the rainbow. A jaguar-skin robe is draped over her shoulders and in one hand is either a long knife or a short spear. She wears a crown made of colorful parrot feathers and long quetzal plumes. An intricate necklace made of gold hangs around her neck, jangling bracelets of gold and silver are on her wrists and ankles, and anklets of jaguar skin rest above her bare feet. There's a glow about her as if she has been lit by some inner light. I don't know what traditional Mayan dress looks like, so I'm not sure where this picture in my mind has just come from. It puzzles me a little bit. What puzzles me even more is why that mental image of her seems to grow and come into clearer focus, so clear that I can see the gold shapes that are linked together in her bracelets and anklets and necklace, and I know what they really are. Each link is a tiny gold skull. And I recognize who she is. The Lady of the Dead.

Sí, I am the Lady, a voice whispers in my head. *I greet you, my little sister.*

I open my eyes and blink. That vision of Corazón is gone and I see her coming down the hallway toward us. Her work clothing is not at all exotic. She has on sensible white tennis shoes and a plain uniform dress, its only decoration the embroidered Mohonk Mountain House logo. Its gray color indicates that she is a member of the serving staff.

The clothes worn by the employees here have different colors and designs according to the different jobs they do. When we first arrived and Dad gave our car keys to the valet he had joked about that with the young man in the green shirt who took our car and the older man in the dark brown shirt who was clearly the younger man's supervisor. "If I wore a purple shirt," Dad said, "would that make me the king?" I guess that doesn't sound so funny when I tell it, but the way my dad said it and the smile he gave them made everyone chuckle.

Corazón has obviously come out to greet us. We've just passed the Winter Lounge and the gift shop and have not yet made the left-hand turn that brings us to the Lake Lounge. We can hear the sound of music being played rather loudly.

"*Buenas noches*," Corazón says. Then she looks back over her shoulder. "It is very crowded in there," she says in a softer voice, "but I have not seen anyone who might be that person you are worried about. Even a costume cannot hide a man's height."

Dad nods. We have told Corazón about the man who abducted them and pretended to be my uncle. We described him as best we could, even though all three of us realized as we did so that it was hard to have a clear image of what he really looked like in our minds. And that is strange because we all have a good memory for faces. All we could remember was that he was far from being a young man, though he didn't move as if he were elderly. He had a kind of energy about him that was intense. He was tall, tall enough to have been a basketball player, with long thin arms and legs and very big hands. There was something about him that looked Indian, but it was hard to define, as hard as it was to describe his features except to say that they were bony and skull-like.

Corazón is holding a serving tray out to us with small loaves of bread on it.

"Take one," she says, "and bite into it. But do not bite hard, *sí*?"

Even though we ate only an hour ago, those little loaves look good to me. They are still warm from the oven. I bite into one and my teeth strike something. I reach into my mouth and pull it out. It is a small white plastic skeleton.

13

Darkness

Dad and Mom and I are in the Lake Lounge now. Just as Corazón said, it is packed with people. Except for the servers, everyone is in costume, both grown-ups and kids. Some are just wearing premolded masks that cover their heads. After all these years, it seems, Richard Nixon is still as popular as Dracula or the Wolf Man or Jason from *Friday the 13th.* But others are wearing really elaborate costumes. Because this is a blend of Halloween and the Mexican Day of the Dead, there are zombies and Zorros, witches and Spanish señoritas, robots and banditos. There's been some research done. I see someone wearing a sign around her neck identifying her as La Llorona, the wailing woman of Mexican folklore. A handsome-looking man in conquistador garb and a woman whose knee-length dark hair has to be a wig are telling everyone within earshot that they are Hernando Cortés and La Malinche, the Indian woman who was his interpreter and ally during the conquest of Mexico.

I'm finding it all kind of amusing and confusing at the same time. In part that is because I am trying to stick like glue to my dad's side and not let go of my mother's hand. It is also because, like my parents, I keep scanning the crowd for a man who is a head taller than everyone else. And there's a third reason for my feeling of disquiet.

It's not what you think, though. It is not that little skeleton I found in my piece of bread. No, that wasn't a mean trick played on me by Corazón. That special bread was what Mexican people call *pan de muerto*, or the bread of the dead. It is considered to be good luck to be the one who bites into the small toy skeleton hidden inside the loaf. The fact that the little loaves taken by my mother and father had nothing in them was a sign of how lucky I had been in choosing that piece. That little plastic skeleton was in my pocket now.

The reason I am feeling uneasy is hard to explain. I guess it started when I saw the first person in a skeleton costume. It wasn't *him*. That person was way too short and the costume was just a body suit with skeletal bones painted on it. But it gave me a start.

I look back over my shoulder and catch the eye of Corazón, who has been moving about the room with her serving tray. She is acting as another set of eyes for us, helping us keep watch. She smiles and then shakes her head. She hasn't seen anything for us to worry about. At least not yet. Still, I feel a sudden cold chill, as if a little of the early winter wind has just blown across my neck.

A feeling is growing inside me that something is very wrong, but I don't know what it is. I turn to look out the window. Spotlights are shining on the new snow and everything is almost as clear as day. That's encouraging. I'm not usually afraid of the dark, but tonight I don't want to look out and see nothing but darkness, a darkness that might hide something that is coming closer with every hidden step. I'm glad it is brightly lit inside this room. Bright enough for me to see anything or anyone that might be a danger to us.

What a crazy thought. There's no reason for me to be so uptight. But I don't let go of my mom's hand and I keep looking around. Then I see something that seems out of place—a person across the room, sitting in a chair near one of the doors that leads out onto the porch. His costume is weird. I can't tell what he is supposed to be. He's wearing a heavy coat, and a ski mask is covering most of his head. But he also has some kind of contraption on top of his head that looks like really complicated binoculars. He slowly lifts a long hand up to brush snow off his shoulder. He's just come in from outside. It must have been when he slipped into the room that I felt that cold breeze on my neck. He looks in my direction, then reaches that long hand up to pull those binoculars down over his eyes like goggles. Is he supposed to be dressed as a space alien?

I squeeze my mom's hand harder, pulling on it to turn her around to see what I'm seeing. She squeezes my hand back to reassure me but doesn't turn. She's leaning up to say something to my dad, who is also not paying attention to what I see. I reach for his belt with my other hand.

"Dad," I try to whisper. But my throat is so dry and tight that all I can do is croak and he doesn't hear me. He's too busy listening to Mom.

The man with the binocular eyes is staring

right at me. I can't see his mouth under that ski mask, but I think he is grinning now. He waves his hand at me and then reaches into his coat pocket to pull out something that looks like a cell phone. Then he begins to stand up, unfolding himself from his chair, and I can see how thin he is, how very tall he is. I want to scream, but I can't.

He holds that cell phone up and then, with his other hand, he presses the buttons. Once, twice . . . and there is the muffled sound of a distant explosion. The lights flicker and everything is plunged into total darkness.

14

Help

I can hear the sound of water dripping but I can't see anything. I seem to be lying on the ground. My head is spinning and aches horribly. I try to lift my hands up to my forehead, but they seem to be caught behind my back. I struggle to free them and realize that my wrists are stuck together. How did this happen? I'm not thinking clearly. I try to remember and the effort is too much for me. I feel as if a hole is opening up underneath me and I'm slipping into it. Just before I drop back into an unconscious state I realize that my hands are tied and that I've been taken captive—and that I know who my captor is.

Help, I whisper, just before I fall into total darkness. *Help me.*

I open my eyes again. This time I can see. Whatever was covering my eyes is gone. So is the sound of dripping water. I don't know

where I was before, but I know it is not where I am now. I'm no longer afraid. Strange as it sounds, I feel peaceful. I'm somewhere down in the earth and there is gold all around me. I don't mean the color gold. I mean real gold. The walls, the floor, even the ceiling of this place is made up of veins of pure gold.

But seeing it this way, I don't feel like I'm looking at riches. I feel as if I am looking at the bones of Mother Earth, seeing them as they should be seen, hidden away. I remember reading about how some Mexican Indians believe that digging gold from the earth always hurts the land, that it is a source of strength when it remains where it is, that we humans were only meant to use whatever gold we find washed out to us in the streams. And that we should then use it only to make things of beauty, because it is a blessing.

"Little Sister," a voice says from behind me, "I am glad that your heart understands this."

I know that voice. It's Corazón. I turn to look and know something else right away. I am in one of my dreams. For instead of a short Mayan woman in her twenties wearing the inconspicuous clothing of a hotel employee, the figure that stands—or, rather, floats—before me is in no way either small or ordinary. She is the exact image that had come to my mind at the party when I tried to imagine Corazón in traditional garb. From the quetzal-plumed crown on her head to the jaguar-skin robe and the anklets of gold, she is the image of someone who is more than an ordinary human being.

I don't ask her who she is. I know that she is the one who loves children, who opens that bridge between those who breathe and those who have passed from this life.

"Little Sister," she says again. Her lips are not moving, but I hear her voice, spoken inside my head. "I have come to help you against the evil one who seeks to do you harm. He thinks this Day of the Dead is his time for revenge. He thinks he will gain power from this time when the darkness of night grows stronger. But he is wrong. He is no friend of either the living or the ancestors. He will get no help from *los muertos*."

Her breathless words give me hope. But I wonder why she is the one who has come into my dreams to help me. Where is the rabbit that has been my guide in the past?

The Lady smiles. It is a smile that doesn't just end at her face but continues to send a glow of warmth that fills the air and touches me and gives me energy. "Little Sister," she says, "your friend is known to our people, too. We know him as the quick little one who can be killed by the touch of a stick yet uses his wits to defeat those who are greater in strength. He is a great helper. It is good that Rabbit has chosen to be your friend."

She gestures around her. "This time, though, I am the one who has come to help. This is my time, my season, and this festival is mine. Even though they do not fully understand what they are doing, those who have brought this festival here have summoned me." She smiles again and drifts closer to me. "Yes, in human miles it is a long way from Mexico. But this is all one land, and the heartbeat of the earth, *el latido del corazón de tierra*, sounds everywhere."

The Lady reaches down a hand to touch me. "You will wake up now," she says. "You will know what to do. Your enemy's weakness is his own thirst for revenge. I do not promise you success, but I promise you the chance to succeed if you behave with courage. Adios."

She lifts her hand from my shoulder and, with a sudden flicker like when a movie ends and the theater goes dark, she and the place where she stood—or floated—are gone.

I'm awake. Really awake this time. I'm not in some groggy semiconscious state or in a dream. I can hear water dripping again and it is still dark because something is over my head. I'm covered by a heavy blanket and my wrists are still tied.

It all comes back to me then, everything that happened when the lights went out. The sky had been clouded over, so there was no glow from the moon or the stars, just deep, deep dark. There was a moment's silence and then chaos. Kids were yelling—some screaming in panic and others just yelling because that is what little kids do when all the lights go out. People were shouting at one another, some telling everyone to be calm, others calling out the names of their children or their husband or their wife. People were pushing and someone fell in between me and Mom and I lost her hand. I reached for my father's belt, but it wasn't there.

I was being moved one way and then another by the surge of the crowd. It was like being caught in a riptide. But that was not the worst part. I knew that somewhere in this panicked human wave there was one being who was as calm and focused as a great white shark. I knew who had caused the lights to go out. What he had held in his hands must have been not a cell phone but a device somehow used to knock out all of the power to Mohonk Mountain House, including any backup generators. And those binocular-like things he had pulled down over his eyes were not part of a costume. I now recognized them as night-vision goggles, because my dad had a pair. While everyone else was blind, Skeleton Man could see.

I knew he was coming toward me and I knew I had to hide. I fell to my knees and crawled through the crowd of confused people, hoping that I had dropped out of his sight. I remembered seeing a table nearby and hoped I was going in the right direction. When my head hit the table leg hard I knew I'd found it. I was half-stunned and worried that I'd cut myself and that blood was dripping down my forehead, but I still pulled myself under the table as far as I could and hoped I was hidden.

But I wasn't.

Two hard, bony hands fastened on my shoulder and pulled me forward. I tried to strike out, but a terribly strong, bony arm wrapped around me, pinning my arms to my sides. I started to scream for help, but my scream was cut off by a moist cloth that was pressed over my mouth and my nose and after that there was nothing to remember other than that last moment of terror, knowing that I had been taken captive by Skeleton Man.

Until now. Until waking up to the sound of water dripping. I move just a little bit to curl myself into a ball. Then I pause. I don't sense anyone watching me, but he might be here. *Listen*, I think. *Listen*. I listen hard, but I don't hear anything other than *drip, drip-drip, drip, drip-drip*, the sound of melting snow falling on stone.

I decide it's safe to move. I bring my knees up as far as I can and thrust my bound hands down below my heels. I have to rock back and forth and it's really hard because my ankles are taped together too. But there's just enough room and I manage to squeeze my legs through and thrust them back. Now my hands are in front of me and I can bring them up to my mouth. There is another piece of tape over my mouth. It hurts, but I manage to peel the tape halfway off with my fingers. And now I can get at the tape around my wrists with my teeth. I find a loose edge and pull, then spit it out, grab again, and pull. I'm unwrapping it only an inch at a time and the taste of the tape is making me feel sick, but I don't stop. I keep at it. *Grab, pull, spit.* There's nothing else in my world but my teeth and this tape around my wrists. I can't stop, because I don't know how long I have before Skeleton Man comes back.

At last I get down to the final wrap. It is stuck so hard to the skin of my wrists that it burns as I pull it free, but I don't even pause. I reach down to my ankles and unwind the tape from them as well. They aren't as tightly wrapped as my hands were. Maybe Skeleton Man ran out of tape. Maybe he wasn't as totally prepared as he thought he was. Maybe he had underestimated me again, as he did when I escaped him the first time.

But I don't throw the blanket off right away. There is a little hole in it and I put my eye up to it and look. I can see through it just enough to make out where I am. It looks like a cave with a tunnel leading into darkness. Someone, and I know who that someone is, has been using this place for quite a while. There's a cot against one wall with a Coleman lantern next to it, and a hot plate and containers of food. To one side of the cot are shelves piled with wires and boxes and electronic equipment. The equipment is connected by a cable to several large storage batteries on the floor. There's a table on the other side of the cot, close to the mouth of the tunnel. A cell phone is sitting on that table. My cell phone. If I get it, I can call my parents, call for help.

But before I can move to throw off the blanket, I hear the scrape of a boot against rock. And through the hole in my blanket I see a ski-masked face wearing a pair of night-vision goggles appear in the mouth of the tunnel. Skeleton Man has returned.

15

In the Cave

The tall, gaunt figure takes three slow steps, moving like a heron stalking its prey in the shallows, ready to strike at any movement. I freeze under the blanket. As he reaches up to take the night-vision goggles from his head, I quickly push the tape back over my mouth, grab the stuck-together ball of tape I've stripped from my wrists and ankles, and thrust my hands behind my back. He is taking the ski mask off now. For a moment it seems as if the face he is uncovering is that of a skeleton, nothing but white bone.

But then I see that he has human features, that his face is the same face I have seen before. It is the harsh, sharp-featured countenance of a man who might be called old, were it not for that awful vitality in his eyes, the intensity in the set of his hard mouth. I quickly close my own eyes as he leans toward me, reaching out one hand to pull the blanket off my face.

"Hunnhhh," he growls. "Still out cold?"

I feel his fingers grasp my cheek and pinch hard, but I will myself not to react. He hasn't pulled the blanket down far enough to see that my ankles are no longer taped together. He doesn't notice that the hands I'm holding behind my back are now free. The blanket is thrown over my head again. It's dusty and some of the dust gets into my nose. It is hard, so hard, not to sneeze. But somehow I manage to control myself, to keep breathing as slowly as someone in a drugged sleep.

I can hear him moving things around. I can't see through the hole in the blanket now, but I'm not even going to try. I have to stay still. I have to wait for a chance to escape, and this is not it.

The sounds tell me that he is still moving about. I don't know how long I was unconscious. Here inside the cave I can't tell if it is day or night. But my hope is that it is night, late at night. So late that, after all his exertion, he's tired.

I direct my thoughts to him: *You are tired, you are very tired. You need to rest. Go to sleep, go to sleep.*

When I finally hear the sound I am waiting for, I almost sigh in relief. It is the creak of the springs of the cot. Then I hear two thuds and see in my mind's eye the boots he has pulled from his feet resting on the cave floor. The cot creaks again as he stretches out on it. I hold my breath, listening even harder. He is rolling back and forth, getting comfortable, and now his breathing is turning into a snore. I think he is asleep.

I begin to move, bringing my hands back around, pulling the blanket down from my face, just a finger's width at a time. I can see him now. He is sleeping on his side, his face turned away from me. I roll to my knees and begin to crawl across the floor of the cave.

The thought goes through my head that I should do something to him, try to knock him out, try to tie him up as he did to me. But I don't see anything I could hit him with and I have this feeling, more than a feeling, that if I tried, I would fail. He would wake up and grab me. I have to head for that tunnel. It must be the way out. I get up off my knees, the blanket still over my shoulders, and keep moving. I move slowly, the way my father taught me to move when you are stalking an animal. I don't tiptoe, but I lift my feet and put them down carefully, rolling from instep to heel with each step. As I pass the table, I reach out and pick up my cell phone with one hand and Skeleton Man's night-vision goggles with the other.

For just a moment his breathing deepens and his snoring becomes words. I freeze in midstep.

"No, not yet," he growls in his sleep. "When she is awake and can see my face. Then . . . It will be painful, yes. Piece by piece, yes. I will have my revenge piece by piece."

Then his words turn into a snarl that makes the hair stand up on the back of my neck, for it is not like the sound a human being should make. It makes me think of some huge, ravenous animal ripping at the flesh of its kill. But he doesn't roll over or sit up, and his breathing again turns into a low snore. I start moving.

When I reach the mouth of the tunnel, I quicken my pace. The passageway is dimly lit by lanterns placed every hundred feet or so. I don't look at those lights. When you move through darkness, you should never look at a light, for it will lessen your perception. But as I pass each lantern I turn it out so that the darkness I leave behind will be that much deeper and maybe that much harder for him to make his way through to follow me when he wakes up.

The passageway is very long. In all the reading I've done over the last few days about the Shawangunk Mountains, I've found no mention of a cave like this, and I wonder how he found it. Is it a place where he's been before? And if so, how long ago was it when he was here last? A year ago, ten years, or at a time when he was one of those monsters that the Lenape people warned their children about in the time before the coming of the Europeans? Another hundred feet, another lantern. I'm climbing now as the floor of the passageway slopes up. There are no more lanterns, but I don't have to put on the night-vision goggles. A circle of light glows from the mouth of the cave ahead of me, and beyond that is the glitter of snow-covered earth.

When I step outside I see that the clouds have cleared from the sky. It is cold, but not the cold of deep winter. I'm warm enough with this blanket around my shoulders. The full moon is shining down. I've never welcomed the sight of the moon more than I do right now.

"Thank you, Grandmother," I say to the

...n a soft voice. As I smile at it, it seems I can see more clearly than ever before the shape that our old people remind us can sometimes be seen on the moon's face. It is Rabbit, who leaped up there long ago. He's looking down and helping me too.

I'm not sure where I am. There are thousands of acres in the Shawangunk range with no roads, just foot trails leading through the forest, up and down the ridges and cliffs. But I do see how I was brought here. Parked in front of the mouth of the cave is a bone-white four-wheel-drive all-terrain vehicle. It's the first one I've seen since we came to Mohonk. Motorized vehicles like snowmobiles and ATVs are strictly forbidden in the Mohonk Preserve. But the cover of the storm must have made it possible for him to sneak this in. The cave is at the bottom of a cliff that rises above me. Tracks in the snow lead back from the cliff down into the woods.

I've driven ATVs before. But when I look close at this one, I see I'm not going to go anywhere on it. The key is gone from the ignition. It must be in Skeleton Man's pocket.

I lift up my cell phone, thinking I can find out if my parents are okay and tell them I need help. I notice that the little phone seems even lighter than usual and I open up the back of it. The battery has been taken out.

And that is when I hear an angry, awful shriek from inside the cave. Skeleton Man has woken and discovered that I'm gone.

16

The Cliff

When the glaciers receded from here fourteen thousand years ago, they left behind a landscape of cliffs and valleys and peaks. Over the centuries, massive chunks of rock fell off the mountains to make huge piles of stones. Those talus piles are everywhere in the Shawangunk range. Rock climbers come from all over the world to scramble through the stones and scale the sheer rock cliffs. Mom and I had taken the trail across Rhododendron Bridge onto Undercliff Carriage Road a day ago to watch some of them working their way up the Trapps Cliffs. They were so high up that on their climbing ropes they looked like tiny spiders, strung together by thin strands of web.

The memory of watching those climbers may seem like a strange thing to have going through my mind now. A part of me wants to run as fast as I can. But running would not be a good idea. I don't know the trails here and I am sure he does. I can't use the ATV, but I'm sure he has the key and can use it to pursue me. I wish I had a knife so I could cut the tires. I don't have time to open it up and do something to the engine.

But I do have another way to go. Up.

I tie the blanket around my neck and start scrambling up the huge stones that lay around the mouth of the cave, concealing it from the sight of any casual passerby. The snow makes the rocks slippery, but my moccasins are the real old-time kind, with one exception. When my mother made them, she built in arch supports and glued on durable soles that have a good tread on them. They are not just made for dress but for dancing or walking—or climbing.

I've climbed at least seventy feet before he comes out of the cave. I'm not looking back over my shoulder or down. It isn't wise to do either when you are climbing by daylight and even more foolish when you have only moonlight to show you where to find hand- and footholds. But I just know he is there. I can feel his hungry, inhuman eyes staring up at me. It is a good thing I can sense him there, because the scream that comes from his throat is so eerie, so piercing, that it might otherwise have shocked me into missing a handhold, losing my grip, and falling.

"Aaaaaarrryyyyaaaaahhhh!"

It sends a chill down my back that is much colder than the feel of the stone cliff on my bare hands. I freeze for just a second. The night-vision goggles that are perched on my forehead slip off and fall down the slope. I hear them strike rock and shatter. But I don't lose my balance or my focus and I start climbing again.

Something hits the cliff next to my face with a hard *thwack*, sending a sharp shard of stone across my cheek. I scramble up even faster and the next softball-size stone that he throws hits near my feet, the third strikes an arm's length beneath me. The fourth hits even lower than that. I think I'm out of his range now, but I don't slow up. If one of those stones had struck me, it would have knocked me loose, like a little bird struck by the spin of a throwing stick. From this height, I would not have survived a fall like that. Skeleton Man is not trying to catch me—now he wants to kill me.

The thing about rock climbing, though, is that you really can't hurry. If you do, you make mistakes. You have to be sure of your holds, certain that you haven't wedged your foot on a shelf of rock that is loose, and grasp firmly before you try to pull yourself up. We have a new climbing wall at our school and I've spent more than my share of time on it. So you might think I would be more sure of myself. But I'm not. I don't have a harness and a line on me. I don't have a chalk bag that I can dip into to keep my hands dry. I'm climbing at night on a rock face that is partially covered with snow. And I haven't even had time to study this cliff I'm scaling, to eyeball it to pick out the best route. I'm climbing blind. But I don't have any other choice.

There are plenty of loose places on this rock face, places where if I put my weight on the flat stone, it would lever out and fall, taking me with it. The thought goes through my mind that it might start a rockfall that would come down on top of him. But it isn't worth the risk if it means I have to go with it. So each time a spot starts to give as I brush away the snow and begin to put my weight on it, I quickly move my hand or my foot to another, safer hold.

Grandmother Moon is helping me. Her light is so bright on the cliff wall that I can see things pretty well. Even the angle of the shadows she casts is just right to show me where I have to put one hand and then the next. I keep making steady progress. I think I am more than halfway to the top. I no longer hear stones striking the wall beneath me. Nor does Skeleton Man let loose another scream of hunger and rage and frustration. And that silence worries me. I begin to wonder if he has a weapon of some kind, like a gun, and if he's getting it out of the ATV now. If he does, will I feel the bullet strike me before I hear the crack of the shot?

What I hear next, though, is not a gunshot. It is the roar of a motor. Skeleton Man has started up the ATV. I pause in my climb to listen as the sound moves away. Then I start climbing again. As much as I hope he's giving up and going away, something inside me says that he isn't. He knows where my climb is going to take me. He is going to cut back around to find the trail that will lead him there. When I get to the top, will Skeleton Man be there waiting for me?

17

The Road

The last fifty feet of my climb are the worst. The cliff begins to slope out and I have to find a way around the small overhang that is above me, that is between me and where I think the top must be. My hands are getting so numb from grasping the snow-chilled rocks that my fingers feel as if they are made of stone themselves. I hold on with one hand and put the other into my armpit. That's the warmest place on your body and it helps restore feeling to my fingers, along with an aching pain so sharp that I almost cry out. I'm feeling exhausted, too, almost too tired to keep hanging on. I have to do something now or I'm going to fall.

Somehow, I don't really understand how, I manage to find a firm enough hold to reach one arm out and up, over the top of that overhang. My fingers find a tree root and I grab hold. It seems firm enough. I can't see it, but I think it is a cedar root. Old cedars grow strong on cliff edges. I feel as if that root is speaking to me, telling me to trust it. I have no other choice. I let go with my other hand, push out and up with my feet, and manage to get my other arm over the top as well to grasp that same friendly root. My feet are kicking at nothing but air. There's a fall of at least a hundred feet below me. I pull, wriggling my body up through snow and twigs and scree. My knees are over the edge now and I'm going hand over hand up that root, which just grows drier and firmer.

My arms wrap around the tree itself. It is as big around as my father's waist and I feel for a moment as if the old cedar tree is holding me just as much as I am holding it. Its rough bark is warm and dry against my cheek and I can smell that aroma that only a cedar has, a clean, faintly sweet scent that makes me think of healing. I remember all the times my dad or my mom and I have sprinkled dry cedar needles on glowing coals and bathed ourselves in the smoke that rose up, cleansing ourselves from all the bad influences that have touched our lives, clearing away sickness, clearing the air. My parents did that for me after the first time I

escaped from Skeleton Man.

That thought takes away whatever sense of safety and security I'd been feeling. Where is he? I listen hard, and to my relief I can still hear the faint growl of an ATV. It continues to move away, not yet going upslope and coming closer. But I can't wait here. There's no time to rest. I have to keep moving. I stand up and brush the snow and dirt from my knees, slip off my moccasins to clean the grit out of them, and slide them back on again. My toes feel numb and I stomp my feet on the ground to try to bring some feeling back into them. Moving. I have to keep moving.

There's a gentle slope ahead of me. It will be easy to climb. But before I go, I place both of my hands on the trunk of the cedar whose root was my lifeline.

"Thank you, Grandfather," I say.

At the top of the slope the ground levels off to a narrow white carpet of snow that extends to my right and my left. It is so level that I know what it must be. I brush away the snow with my foot. It is the surface of a road. I look around and recognize where I am. Although the night and the snow make everything look different, I am on the main road that leads up to the Mountain House, just past the Mountain House Gate.

That road gives me both hope and a deep sense of foreboding. I can follow it back up to where there are people who can protect me. Or I can head back down toward the gatehouse. But I don't know if anyone will be there. At night, I think, they just leave it unattended, especially when there's been a big snowstorm like the one we just had and there's no likelihood of anyone driving up or down. And if I reach the gatehouse and it is all locked up and no one is there, what good will it do me? Who will protect me from Skeleton Man if he tracks me there? I might even run into him coming up the road as I am going down.

But even if I do go up, toward the Mountain House, it won't be easy. I think it is at least a mile. I can't run fast on a road slippery with snow. Skeleton Man may be able to catch up to me before I can reach safety.

I have to decide. As I stand there trying to decide what to do, I can feel myself getting colder. The blanket is still tied around my shoulders, but it is not enough to keep me from developing hypothermia if I stand still. Running—not headlong but at a careful, steady jog—will warm me up and, perhaps, get me to the place I have to reach in time. I turn and start running up the road.

18

The Blade

The snow is not as deep as it was when it first fell. The road surface must not have dropped down to freezing, so the drifts have begun to melt from the bottom. In places where it was swept by the wind, the road is actually clear of snow, but in others there is still as much as six inches with icy patches in between. So I have to run with care. I don't want to fall and hurt myself, maybe twist an ankle. I have to keep going.

The running is warming me up. My breathing has settled into an even, steady rhythm. But I'm far from relaxed, because I keep listening for a sound from behind me, the sound of the engine of an ATV. Every now and then I catch it as I turn a bend. It is still thin and distant, like the whining buzz of a hornet, but I think it has been growing louder and closer. My feet thump on the road surface, then slosh through snow that is wet and heavy and pulls at my moccasins. I slip and almost fall, but I manage to catch myself with my hands and keep running.

The back of my left hand is hurting, though. I glance at my knuckles. The moonlight is bright enough to see a dark flow welling out from a cut. I don't know when that happened. Maybe it was when I was climbing and my hands were too numb to feel it, too cold to bleed freely. My near tumble has just opened it enough for the blood to start dripping out. There's a deep pocket in my buckskin dress and I reach into it with my other hand to pull out a Kleenex that I'd wadded in there. I wrap it over my bleeding knuckle. It's not that it is cut deeply enough for me to lose enough blood to weaken me. A knuckle cut doesn't bleed all that much. It is that I don't want to leave a blood trail behind me. Even though the logical part of my mind knows that the man who posed as my uncle and took me captive is just an evil human being, another part of my mind knows with equal certainty that he is more than that. He is a monster, the kind of monster that can smell blood.

I wish that I was the one on the ATV and

that he was the one on foot. It's not right. In the old stories the monsters don't use machines. It isn't fair. Yes, I know it is crazy for me to think of this when I'm running for my life. But exhaustion and fear can bring thoughts into your head that don't make logical sense, like feeling there has to be some better way for me to escape other than on foot.

Then, as I see a familiar cutoff in the road and a pile of earth and stone ahead of me at the cliff's edge, I realize that my thoughts are logical after all. I jog off the road to the bulldozer I had spotted the other day. On the radiator grille is a word that my dad spelled out for me when I was four years old and visiting a job site with him for the first time: INTERNATIONAL. That word brings a smile to my face. I know this big yellow machine. My dad taught me all about it.

There's not much snow on the bulldozer, which had clearly not quite finished its work on the road before the snowstorm hit. It is still sitting here, ready to go. I step up onto the push arm and then the track to get into the cab. It isn't a really big bulldozer, but it is big enough for me to feel protected by it as I step over the steering levers and sit down on the black padded seat. It is completely dry inside. I run my hands over the controls of the big machine, reminding myself what is what. The blade control lever is to the side of the right armrest, the decelerator—no, the brake pedal—is under my right foot. I put my hands on the two steering levers, which are between my legs. Here's the decelerator pedal—under my left foot. Now . . . the engine speed control lever is by my left elbow. Yes. And the transmission shift? Okay, here it is, a foot farther to the left, over the gearbox.

I make sure everything is set, then reach my right hand down to the starter switch.

Baabaaabaabaa-barooooom. The engine catches and then grumbles into life. I feel as much as hear the steady, smooth rumble of the big diesel as it warms up.

The instrument panel is lit now and I flick on the headlights, then work the blade control lever. There's a slight jolt as the lift cylinders pull back and the blade lifts free. I manipulate the lever to shake loose the dirt and snow. It's a good two feet off the ground, high enough so that it won't catch anything, but I can still see over it.

I push forward on the right steering lever, pull back on the left, and the bulldozer makes a tight pivot. Its headlights illuminate the snow-covered road that leads toward the Mountain House. Those lights also reflect off the bone-white finish of the ATV that has just pulled up to block my way. In the stark gleam of the headlights I can see the tall, thin figure astride that ATV, his head a glistening skull, his eyes red as blood.

19

Cat and Mouse

"Aaaaaarrryyyyaaaaahhhh!"

Skeleton Man stares into the bright glare of the bulldozer's headlights. He has raised himself up from the seat and is standing on the ATV. He is just about to get off. He'll be on me in half a dozen strides of his long legs. The sound of the diesel motor of the bulldozer is so loud that I didn't hear his approach. I'm frozen at the controls.

But I stay frozen for only a heartbeat. I haven't climbed and run this far to get caught like a foolish little mouse backed into a corner by a cat. Not when this mouse has several tons of steel under her, steel controlled by an engine with as much power as a herd of horses. I shift into reverse, and the bulldozer rolls backward as I work the steering levers to keep my enemy in the beam of the headlights. I hear the familiar *beep-beep-beep-beep* warning sound that echoes through

every construction site whenever some big piece of machinery starts backing up. I love that sound, and right now it makes me feel as if it is the voice of this huge yellow beast I'm riding.

"Come on, baby," I say to the bulldozer as I steer her backward in a half circle. "Let's show him what you've got."

I can tell that I've surprised Skeleton Man. He probably hadn't expected a kid to be able to run a dozer. Instead of getting off the ATV, he settles back into the seat, grips the handlebars, and revs the engine so hard that when he pops the clutch it roars forward into a wheelie. But as soon as he gets close enough, I stop, shift, and roll forward even faster than I went back. Skeleton Man has to turn sharply and speed up to avoid getting hit by the blade of the dozer.

"Yes!" I say.

I'm not frightened now. There is so much adrenaline pumping through me that I feel as if I could make my big yellow metal horse take flight. I pull the left steering lever back and push forward on the right. The bulldozer spins in a tight circle so that I keep Skeleton Man in the beam of the headlights. Every time the lights catch him, he raises a bony hand to block his eyes from their glare and I can't see his full face. But what I do see makes me swallow hard. He doesn't seem at all human anymore—he's just a glaring, red-eyed skull.

It's like a dance now. Each time he tries to get close I back up, turn, roar forward, turn again to evade his approach. I'm not certain what he thinks he'll be able to do. He must know that he can't get off his much smaller machine to try to attack me on foot. There's no way he's going to scale the treads of a moving bulldozer. I turn, go forward, back up, spin, drive forward again.

Our game of cat and mouse continues. Though it is more like lion versus elephant, I think. Then it comes to me. His plan isn't really to get close enough to catch me. He's trying to get me to make a mistake, stall out, or even run out of fuel. Then he can leap up into the cab and grab me like an owl sinking its claws into a baby bird. I'm safe only as long as I don't do something wrong. As soon as I think that, my wet moccasin slips off the pedal. I lurch forward out of control for a second before I manage to get my foot back in place again, my heart pounding at the thought of him catching me.

Suddenly I know—I'm seeing it wrong. I'm not the mouse. I'm the cat. I shouldn't be evading him. I should be on the attack. As quickly as

I realize this, I act. I lower the blade, shift, push the throttle to its highest point, and pop my feet off the pedals. My yellow behemoth doesn't just roll forward, it seems to almost jump through the air. And it takes Skeleton Man totally by surprise. He tries to turn his ATV, but he's too late. The blade catches the side of his four-wheeler. As I raise the blade, it lifts him and his ATV up into the air.

But I've been so intent on catching my enemy off guard that I haven't noticed where I am. I'm heading right toward the edge of the cliff! I ram the pedals to brake just as one side of the bulldozer blade hits the edge of a huge slab of rock.

Ker-whomp!

The sound of the blade hitting that huge stone is like an explosion. It's helped me stop, but it jolted me so hard that I've been thrown forward against the steering levers. The breath has been knocked out of me and I feel as if my ribs are cracked. But I can't think of that now. I slam my feet back down on the decelerator and the brake to keep from crawling forward again just as a terrible scream fills the air.

"Aaaaaarrryyyyaaaaahhhh!"

Skeleton Man and his ATV were flipped forward off the blade of the bulldozer when we struck that stone. In the beam of the headlight

I see him there at the cliff's edge, the machine on top of him as he windmills his long arms, screaming as he tries to get free.

"Aaaaaarrryyyyaaaaahhhh!"

Then the earth collapses beneath him. He and the four-wheeler fall over the edge. That huge stone I struck, which is twice the size of the bulldozer, also begins to slide. Half of the mountain slope and a big chunk of the road edge in front of me goes with it.

For a second the whole world is filled with the rumble and roar of a landslide. The bulldozer shakes beneath me and I wonder if the road is going to collapse under us. But then, as suddenly as it began, it is over. As the last echoes die away, all is quiet aside from the rattle of a few stray rocks falling.

I take a deep breath. Then, holding my side, I climb off the yellow bulldozer. I leave it in neutral with its motor running, just in case. But when I get to the edge of the crumbled cliff, I can feel in my heart there's nothing to fear now. Grandmother Moon is shining her light even brighter than before on the white stones of the talus slope. She shows me that Skeleton Man is gone. He is down there somewhere, buried forever under thousands of tons of rock.

20

By the Fire

A hand grasps my shoulder.

"More hot cocoa, Molly?" my mom asks. Dad is leaning over her to hold out a plate of cookies. It's teatime at Mohonk and we're sitting in the Lake Lounge by the fire, the same room where the lights went out two nights ago and Skeleton Man took me away. We've had to stay here an extra two days because of the investigation, but we've managed to make most of it feel like a vacation. It hasn't been hard to enjoy ourselves now that the sense of foreboding that hung over us like a sword on a thin thread is gone.

"Thanks," I say. I reach out one bandaged hand for the cocoa and grab three cookies with the other. My parents both laugh.

"Well," I say, "I'm hungry." That makes them laugh harder and I laugh with them, even though laughing makes my bruised ribs hurt.

As we sit and look at the fire, it seems as if all the scary and awful things that just happened occurred ages ago. My fears that my parents had been hurt turned out to be groundless. That night when Skeleton Man killed all the power on the mountain, I was the only person he attacked. I'm sure he had further plans, but we'll never know what they were.

They haven't been able to find any trace of his body, though they did find some pieces of the shattered ATV at the bottom of the slope. The stones that slid down are too big for anyone to move and the state troopers say that we might as well think of it as the grave of the unidentified man who kidnapped me. From what I told them and from the way he operated, they agreed it might very well have been the same person who kidnapped my mom and dad and posed as my uncle a year ago. But with no hard evidence other than what I said I saw, that remains only a theory as far as they are concerned.

But what about that cave and all his stuff, you ask? They listened to my description of that place and they've searched for it. But the snow had all melted away by the time they started looking and they couldn't even find the tracks of the ATV. So far they haven't been able to find the cave either. I'm not sure how hard they've tried. Apparently everyone who knows anything about this area says there is no such cave that anyone else has ever found. I was probably in shock and remembered it wrong—or at least that's what they theorize. I even told them about the cedar tree whose roots helped me climb those last few feet over the cliff, but they claim there are no cedar trees growing along that stretch of road at all, and never have been.

Some things can never be explained. One of them is Corazón. My mom and I both remember meeting her and talking with her. I know she was my friend. Her face was one of those I looked for in the crowd of people gathered inside Mohonk when I came walking up the snowy road that night—well, more limping than walking. And I think I did see her at the edge of the light from the flashlights. She was dressed again in those beautiful traditional Mayan clothes.

I saw her smile at me, put her hand on her heart, and mouth words that I am sure were *net tsoi.* I'd never heard those words before, but somehow I knew they meant "all is good" in

Mayan. Then Mom and Dad were hugging me so hard that all I could see or think about was how happy I was that we were all together and safe. When I looked around again, Corazón was nowhere to be seen.

But yesterday, when Mom and I went looking for Corazón after I'd finished my first interviews with the state troopers, we couldn't find her. And when we asked, we were told that there was no one by that name employed by the Mohonk Mountain House. Mom and I just looked at each other when we heard that. Then Mom finally told me the proverb that Corazón had shared with her. "Take heart when you feel lost, for a friend may find you."

So, that's the end of my story. I'm the girl who got away from a monster not just once but twice. Even though they say that lightning doesn't strike twice, I know now that it does. I know that just as surely as I know that love and courage are strong enough to defeat hatred and greed.

And I also know Skeleton Man is gone again from our lives. This time, I hope, he is gone for good.